VICTORIA VILLALOBOS

VENGEANCE

BOOK 2

STEVE PAGE

Library of Congress Control Number: 2023917575

26 25 24 23 22 21 20 19 18 17 1 2 3 4 5

ISBN-13 (Ebook): ISBN: 978-1-958716-04-5

ISBN-13 (Paperback): ISBN: 978-1-958716-05-2

ISBN-13 (Hardcover with Dust Jacket): ISBN: 978-1-958716-06-9

ISBN-13 (Case Laminate): ISBN: 978-1-958716-07-6

ACKNOWLEDGMENTS

To my best friend and lover, Nikki, you have been an inspiration and motivation to stay the course to completion. Thank you for always believing that there is greatness in me, especially when I doubt it myself. You are my biggest cheerleader and motivator. You set the bar for work ethic and passion which is something to aspire to.

To my editor and the greatest fan of the story, you have been invaluable in moving the story along and helping ensure the questions are answered, even if they take longer to reveal than you would like. Your impatience to learn what is going to happen has made me push to create a cohesive and captivating story.

To my friends, who have not only encouraged this project but have provided the mental breaks needed to feed creativity, thank you. Please keep the crazy going, I can't wait for our next adventure.

CHAPTER 1
SITREP

Let's recap. Vic's mission of avenging her cousin's death by making his killer pay has been mostly successful thus far. Gregario, the man responsible for Richie's death and the head of the Gulf Cartel, is in her custody. With some intense persuasion and a few clues, she has been able to refresh Gregario's memory and he now knows the reason for his capture. Although he remembers her from that day at the beach, he does not know her name or anything about her.

During the capture of Gregario, many key events happened. For the team, the most impactful was the loss of Mark, their grumpy, but always reliable friend. He was one of the best operators and the team will have a hard time finding his replacement. They will have to incorporate a new player fast because they will need all the help they can get for their next op.

With Gregario off the radar, Marco, his second in command, has taken over as head of the Gulf Cartel. There was chatter of the search for Gregario for a short time, but the chatter mysteriously stopped. Until the close of Part 1, Vic's team did not know why everyone went silent regarding the disappearance of Gregario.

In addition to the death of Mark, a few key players in the organized crime world met their demise. The Serbian Mafia lost not only the head of the organization, Mr. Novak, but also his number two, Goran, who was eliminated. Goran's justice was served by the innocent victims of the human trafficking trade business the Serbians were trying to expand into. Vic's team was able to liberate the captives and return them home. There are a few top members of the Serbian Mafia who are fighting for control but currently, the organization is reeling and trying to hold itself together.

For the Central American Cartel (CAC), Juan Robles was the public face until he too was taken out. Now the question is, will Pablo Arias step out of the shadows and reveal himself as the true head of the organization, or will he find another puppet so he can stay off the radar? Either way, with the human trafficking shipment being intercepted, the CAC must take swift action to save face and reinforce its reputation as the elite force in organized crime.

This brings us to the current dilemma that Victoria and her team face. The final chapter of Part 1 revealed that Leo, the CAC's number two and enforcer, had captured Robby. Camilo was shocked to see his cousin tied to a chair at Leo's side. It was implied that Leo was looking to make a trade, Gregario for Robby. With Gregario in rough shape, it is questionable what condition Robby will be in if the team is able to get him back.

Leo had called Victoria by name as he broke in through what they thought were secure connections. This raises many questions as to how he was able to identify Vic, and how much he knows about the team and their mission. One thing is certain, with what she knows about Leo so far, he is definitely the most formidable opponent she has faced so far.

Is Victoria willing to sacrifice her desire to take Gregario's life in order to save the life of Robby? Even if she does go through with the trade, how will the team be able to pull it off without being wiped out by the many highly trained cartel men? This time, it will be much more difficult because they no longer have the element of surprise. This time, the cartel will know they are coming.

CHAPTER 2
THE CLOCK IS TICKING

"Based on your recent attacks on my organization, I assume you are still hiding out somewhere in Europe," said Leo. "I will give you 48 hours to bring Mr. Gregario to me in Costa Rica. I will send you the location. But first, I need proof of life in the next hour. You will video call me so I may assess his condition. Assuming he is in good health, I will not harm your friend. If his condition worsens, well, let's just say that Robby here will meet a similar fate. I trust your man in Russia can help you with where to send the video."

Leo's feed terminated leaving only Ivan on the screen with a look of great concern on his face. It took a few seconds for them to process what had just happened. Ivan was the first to speak.

"I'm so sorry Vic,... "started Ivan.

"We don't have time for sorry Ivan," Vic's response was not one of hostility but pure business. "You need to figure out how he hacked us, we cannot operate effectively with compromised communications. That is priority number one for you.

"Priya, begin making arrangements for transport to Costa Rica." Vic continued her instruction. "Gregario and the three of us need to get there as soon as possible."

"I told you not to involve him," Camilo started.

"Stow it, Camilo!" replied Vic. "You know I feel terrible this happened, but there will be plenty of time for I told you so's after we get him back. It is going to take all of us to rescue him. I seriously doubt the Central American Cartel will simply trade him for a bloody and bruised Gregario."

Addressing the group, Victoria explained their next move. "We have to get him cleaned up and looking as normal as possible for the video. We have 58 minutes and counting to make him appear to be unharmed. Somehow, we have to convince Gregario that it is in his best interest to cooperate."

"Imri, we need you to help keep Gregario sedated while we prep him. Start working on his wounds. Do whatever you can to minimize their visibility. If he needs stitches, take care of it. Then be ready to put whatever it takes into his IV to get him lucid and feeling as comfortable as possible." she continued.

"Camilo, first I need you to go get as much ice as you can find and fill that 55-gallon drum in the room with Gregario," Vic softened her tone when she addressed him. She knew he was on edge and needed him as focused on the tasks at hand as possible. "We need to give him an ice bath to try to reduce as much swelling as possible. Once you are done with that, I need you to make a list of any operators you can think of that you would trust to help us. Preferably those that are already in Costa Rica. Perhaps some of your friends from the Unidad Especial de Intervención. We need trained operatives, and the UEI's understanding of the terrain would be invaluable."

"I am going to try to set up a suitable backdrop for the call. I think the office on the west side has a blank wall without broken windows. When I am finished there, I will assist Imri with tending to Gregario's wounds and cleaning him up. Once we are done with the ice bath, I am going to grab what little makeup I brought with me and try to put some lipstick on this pig. Hopefully, I can conceal some of the bruising. Fortunately, our skin tones are fairly similar."

"In the meantime, we need to think of any leverage we can use to get him to cooperate. Let's get started, there is no time to waste." Vic terminated the connection and closed the laptop. The team set off to attend to their various tasks.

CHAPTER 3
STITCHES AND SWELLING

Camilo took the van and sped off to the nearest store to buy all the ice they had. It was apparent he was extremely angry with Victoria for getting his cousin involved in this mess, but he is a good soldier and knows when it is best to simply follow orders. Vic was right, if he had any hope of getting Robbie back in one piece, he would need the help of the entire team. As he drove, he searched his mind for the best candidates to join the team on the rescue mission.

Back at the safehouse, Imri grabbed the medical kit from the lockers and headed to the utility room where Gregario was being held. He was not a doctor but had received training from a field medic. It was his job to cover the medic while he treated injured soldiers and civilians. In the process, he got a crash course in medicine.

After checking Gregario's vitals, he put a bit of sedative into his IV. He knew that the ice bath would stimulate Gregario and that the pain from his wounds would potentially cause him to regain consciousness. It was best to keep him knocked out while they tried to disguise the damage they had inflicted on his body. Fortunately, much of their punishment had been in the form of pressure points that did not leave marks.

It didn't take Vic long to move the debris from the room and establish a suitable place for the call. She used the laptop to ensure the signal would be strong enough in the room for the call. Once she was satisfied the location was ready, she moved back to the utility room to help Imri.

When she got there, Imri had already hosed him down and given him a quick sponge bath. He had cleaned the wounds from the lashes to Gregario's back. They were not very deep and did not require stitches. All he could do was apply ointment and dressings.

"I guess the next thing we should do is to get him down from the chains," suggested Imri.

The team had strung up Gregario from chains that hung from the ceiling. Suspending him had been greatly effective in getting information from him and inflicting excruciating pain.

The pain from the bullet hole in Imri's leg kept him from being able to function at full strength. Vic helped him lower Gregario to the floor and dragged him to the dentist's chair in the center of the room. After they applied the restraints, they began working on the wounds on his face.

"This left eye is going to be our biggest issue," said Imri.

Vic nodded in agreement as she looked at the swollen and cut face of Gregario. "

Using the suture kit from the med kit, Imri placed three stitches in the corner of Gregario's eye where it had torn open from the blows. The team had focused on the one eye allowing Gregario to keep a good eye to see what was coming next.

"That's a little better," said Imri as he snipped the thread of the last stitch.

"Here," Victoria said as she pulled the instant ice pack from the med kit and placed it on Gregario's left cheek and eye. "Let's hope this helps."

Victoria and Imri continued to clean wounds and scrub the dried blood from Gregario's body. They were just finishing scrubbing his torso when Camilo entered the room with bags of ice on his shoulders.

"I emptied their cooler," he reported. "They had 15 bags; I hope it is enough."

They all helped unload the van and fill the drum. Once all the ice had been added, Imri grabbed the hose and began filling it the rest of the way with water. Vic and Camilo worked together to drag Gregario and lift him into the drum. His body began to spasm as the ice-cold water stimulated his nervous system.

"We only have 20 minutes of this before we need to get him out and start prepping him," said Vic. "Camilo, have you thought of anyone we can contact to help?"

"Yeah," replied Camilo. "I have a couple of men we can ask but I am not sure if they are available."

"Go contact Ivan and see if he can help track them down. We need to assemble the team ASAP. If they are willing to help, Ivan can help coordinate their involvement."

Camilo nodded at Vic to signal he understood and exited the room. He needed space and at this point, it was best that he didn't have to work side-by-side with Vic. Camilo is not the only one with issues. Victoria is very worried about Robbie and knows she is responsible for what has, and is, about to happen to him. Her guilt makes it difficult to know what to say to Camilo as she tries to lead the team. Separate tasks are the best way for the team to operate efficiently and without conflict.

CHAPTER 4
NOT YOUR AVERAGE SPA DAY

The utility room smelled of metal, oil, and bleach. Condensation formed on the outside of the drum as the metal searched for equilibrium between the ice water inside and the warm air of the room. The boiler on the other side of the wall kept the room quite warm.

The timer on Imri's tactical watch chirped and he looked to Vic.

"Let's get him out," she confirmed.

Pain shot through Imri's injured leg whenever he tried to put weight on it. His face grimaced as the weight of the barrel made him brace while he and Vic gently tipped over the barrel. Together, they pulled Gregario's cold body from the ice and got him strapped into the chair. It was obvious Imri was not in any shape for a closed-quarters battle.

With Gregario restrained, Imri checked his vitals and let Vic know he was stable for her to begin prepping. Vic laid her supplies out on the counter and considered if there was anything else she needed.

"Can you please get my hair dryer from the locker?" she asked.

She knew the walk to the office and back would be painful for Imri, but she didn't have another job for him at the time, and she really needed the hair dryer. She began to dry Gregario's head when her eye caught a glance at the air compressor in the corner. "Screw this," she thought as she grabbed the hose and flipped the compressor on. In moments she had enough pressure to begin drying Gregario's body.

As Vic worked, she considered the swap. She expected to need a minimum of two teams of operators. Imri is a great shot and with his leg injury, he will be best used as overwatch. Camilo and her knew Robby best and were most determined to bring him home safely, they were obvious team leaders. Camilo had reached out to his team members but Vic needed to see who else she could get to help. It was time to contact The Skipper.

She would have to give him a call as soon as she got done with the call with Leo, but first, she needed to focus on the task at hand. If she can get at least a 20% improvement, Robby is in serious trouble. Fortunately, the ice reduced the swelling considerably.

Before long Imri returned with the hair dryer.

"Thanks," said Vic. "Can you take over on the body?" she asked as she reached out the nozzle in his direction.

Imri handed her the hair dryer and took the compressor nozzle from her. Vic plugged the hair dryer into the extension cord and began drying Gregario's face and hair. She wasn't concerned about the hair being dry, but it could not drip and mess up the makeup she was going to apply.

After a couple of minutes, she decides she needs to get to work on covering up the bruising. She trades the dryer for some concealer and a sponge. As she works, she remembers her cousin Richie picking on her when she started putting on make-up to impress the neighbor boy Juan.

Thinking back, she reminisces about the bond they had and how much she misses him.

Gregario has made the connection of why he's in her control. He has experienced a great amount of pain. He has lost a mountain of money. He has received punishment for his transgressions. But is it enough?

If she is still committed to watching him take his last breath, she will have to wait. Robby's life Is more important than taking Gregario's. Perhaps this reprieve will give Gregario's body enough time to recover so that their next encounter will be starting all over again. The pain will be fresh as new wounds are created. Plus, his mind will be consumed with the ones who are hunting him.

Imri finished with the compressor and turned it off. He was so focused on his task he hadn't seen what Vic was doing.

"Wow, that's amazing!" exclaimed Imri as he approached the table.

"You think so?" asked Vic. "Do you think it's enough for the camera?"

"With the lighting in that room, I think it's perfect," Imri answered. "He looks so natural, not too good but it is obvious he's taken a few blows to the face."

"Yeah," replied Vic, "I would expect nothing less than to be beaten a little if I was taken. Anyone who eliminates a security detail to take you doesn't just want to talk."

"Smart," agreed Imri.

"Let's get him dressed and in position," instructed Vic. "You get started preparing to wake him up and I'll go get Camilo to help us get him transferred to the office with the camera set-up."

Vic left Imri to get started and headed for the office to find Camilo.

"Can you he...." Vic started but stopped when she realized the office was vacant. Through the window, she saw Camilo outside talking with a truck driver. They were pointing and nodding until the man smiled and drove around the corner of the building. Vic headed to the door to meet Camilo who was heading in.

"What was that about?" Vic asked as he stepped through the door.

"Just a lost driver trying to deliver some supplies to the factory to the south" answered Camilo.

"Did you talk to Ivan?" she asked.

"Yes, he's working on it," he replied.

"I need you to give me a hand transferring

Gregario." She said as she pointed to the office with the camera.

"Okay," said Camilo without expression. There was a distinct absence of small talk between these two. They said nothing as they made their way through the building to the utility room.

"I've got the injections prepped," said Imri as they entered the room. "We should get them started as soon as possible if you want him lucid for the call."

"Understood," said Vic. "Camilo, you take the right side and I'll take the left." They removed Gregario's restraints and began getting him dressed.

"His shirt has a lot of blood stains," said Imri holding it up for them to see.

"I've got one we can use in my locker," offered Camilo.

"Get it," instructed Vic and Camilo hurried to retrieve it.

When they had finished dressing him, they each put an arm around their necks. Grabbing his wrist and belt they dragged Gregario to the office. The toes of Gregario's leather shoes scuffed as they scraped across the floor. His $20 shine was being ruined.

They tied Gregario's hands to the table and got ready to restore his consciousness. The clock was ticking, and Vic wanted to make sure he would comply.

"Let's wake him up," said Vic. "You can keep him stoned right?"

"Yes," confirmed Imri. "He will be able to talk but may not make much sense. He will be disoriented so I think to avoid too much confusion you should be the only one in the room," he said as he looked at Vic. "I can wait outside and listen. If you need me just say so, and I'll come in."

Camilo took the hint and headed for the door.

When we are done, I will also administer GHB so he won't remember the call."

"So glad you joined the team," said Vic. "Your skills have been priceless."

"Thanks," said Imri who accepted the recognition gracefully.

Since they had to remove the IV for the ice bath, Imri had to inject the drugs. He wrapped the tourniquet around Gregario's arm and found a vein suitable for their needs. He depressed the plunger, removed the tourniquet, and within a minute Gregario began to try to take in his surroundings. Imri swiftly left the room and took up station outside the door.

Gregario's eyes rolled loosely, trying to focus on anything they could recognize as consciousness slowly crept through his mind.

"Don... Donde?" Gregario stammered.

"Where..?

"Quién?..."

She didn't want to spark any memories of his recent encounters, so she spoke to him in their native language Spanish. She paid particular attention to her accent to try to sound more like she was from Mexico like him rather than Costa Rica.

"Do you know who you are?" Vic asked in a plain tone showing no emotion.

"Adolfo Rivera Gregario" he mumbled. The signal between his brain and his mouth struggled.

"Do you know where you are?" she continued.

"Uhh...." Gregario's head rolled as he looked around the room. "No."

She decided to switch from questions to instructions on what was about to happen.

"Mr. Gregario, in a few moments you will receive a video call." She spoke slowly and directly.

"You will be asked a few simple questions. You will be brief in your answers. Do you understand?"

"Uhhh....yes," Gregario acknowledged.

"I'm going to sit right next to you so don't worry. I'll be right here in case you need anything." She tried to assure him she was friendly and that he could trust her. The drugs were working, and he had no idea what was really happening. He gave her a look of slight relief.

On the table in front of them, the screen of the laptop indicated an incoming video call. Victoria held her breath and prayed this call went well.

"Hello, Victoria," greeted Leo.

"Hola," replied Vic hoping Leo would continue the conversation in Spanish as that seemed to be helping keep Gregario unaware of what was going on.

CHAPTER 5
SILK TIES AND LEGOS

"Donde esta Robby," Vic asked where Robby was because Leo was the only one on camera. She wanted to make sure he still looked like he was in good shape.

Leo instinctually replied in Spanish, "He's right here."

The camera panned to the left and Robby could be seen in front of a light green wall, strapped to a chair. There appeared to be light coming from a window to his right. He was gagged and didn't seem to be harmed aside from a bloody lip.

Vic continued speaking in Spanish. "Robby, are you okay?"

Seeing Victoria speaking to him overwhelmed him and Robby began fighting back tears and getting choked up. The stress of the situation was mounting, and he had not been trained for situations like this. He was not prepared and had no coping mechanisms. He was terrified and had no idea what to do.

Robby slowly moved his head as he nodded that he was okay since he could not speak with the gag in his mouth. The camera swung back to Leo's face.

"I see you are not gagged, Mr. Gregario, how are you?" Leo inquired.

"Perfecto," replied Gregario, eyes rolling in his head. It was obvious he was high as a kite.

"I see you have him drugged," said Leo disapprovingly.

"We had other plans before your call," replied Vic. "You caught us in the middle of some good times."

"I see, and apparently you had enough time to have quite a bit of fun based on the looks of Mr. Gregario's eye."

The camera widened as he spoke, and as he finished his sentence, Leo struck Robby with a vicious right. Robby leaned so hard he nearly tipped his chair over. The skill of his strike was so effective it opened a small cut in one blow. Robby was knocked loopy. His head was spinning, and his ears filled with the sound of his heart pounding. The blow had scrambled his thoughts and they were desperately searching for a solid place to re-assemble themselves.

"Hey!" yelled Vic. She knows she should show as little emotion toward Robby, but his breakdown was throwing her off her game a bit. Digging her nails into her thighs under the table, she quickly regained her composure as Leo returned his focus to the camera and screen.

He adjusted his Salvatore Ferragamo tie and straightened his tailored jacket. "Now we are one step closer to even," Leo sneered. "Perhaps my associate can bring your friend Robby here some candy too."

"Please, don't," Vic asked with little emotion. She still needed to protest, just with less conviction. The more Leo knew she cared about Robby the more he would use Robby against her. More cherished meant more pain and suffering for Robby.

"Oh, but it's only fair." Leo scoffed. "Mr. Gregario is very important to us, and you have shown him such a good time, Robby must also have the experience to remember."

A man partially entered the frame and Vic could see he was handing Leo a syringe and tourniquet. Leo quickly administered the needle. Robby's head rolled back, and he passed out.

"Can we get on with the trade?" Vic tried to bring the focus back to the swap rather than on punishing Robby for what they had done to Gregario. She was secretly pleased that Leo had drugged Robby. He might have a bad trip, but he would feel less pain this way. She had to object in order to make Leo feel like it was his idea.

"What are we watching?" asked Gregario. He did not realize it was a video call and he thought it was a television show.

"It is me, Leo," Leo tried to communicate with him. "This is an internet meeting. Do you remember me, sir?"

"Leo?" Gregario's expression showed he knew the name, but his mind was lost, searching for the connection.

Leo recognized it was useless to try to get any reliable information from him at this point. "Begin your travels for Robby's resort," he instructed Vic.

"Once you are there, you will receive coordinates and the time of the trade."

"I understand," Vic confirmed.

"When we meet, he better be in better condition than he is right now," warned Leo. "Do you understand what I am saying?"

"Yes," Vic was very direct.

Leo did not waste any more time and the signal terminated. Ivan immediately rang in. Vic accepted the connection and greeted him. "Did you get all that?"

"Yep," replied Ivan. He had been monitoring the feed. "Priya arranged your flight, and you should head to the airport as soon as possible. The plane is waiting. I will scrub the video to make sure we didn't miss anything, but I don't expect to find anything. I'll also try to backtrace the signal."

"Good," responded Victoria. "Have you found a way to secure our comms, or do we still have a hole in the fence? I don't want Leo knowing our every move before we make it."

"Yes," sighed Ivan. "I was able to identify the path in and was able to close the port. I've updated the encryption and rewrote the code for the algorithm. It is much stronger now."

"Keep checking for weaknesses and keep

digging," instructed Vic. "We need to find some leverage and a way to get ahead of the CAC"

Hearing Ivan's voice, Camilo and Imri rounded the door frame and entered the room. They leaned against the wall and listened in on the briefing.

"I was able to liaise with Camilo's connections in Costa Rica," Ivan continued to report on recent developments. "They will be ready when you get there."

"Thanks, bro," said Camilo"

"No problem," answered Ivan. Turning back to Vic he asked, "Have you given any thought to who you want to have your back out there?

"I have another call to make as soon as we are done here." She answered. "I'm hoping The Skipper will know how to reach a few operators."

"Let me know if Priya or I can help." Ivan offered.

"I always do," replied Victoria as she signed off.

Vic got up from her seat and addressed the men. "Camilo, you, and I will get this piece of shit back to the utility room. Imri, collect the gear and take it to the office and begin prepping for transport. When we are finished Camilo will join you and I will follow once I'm done with my call."

"Roger that," the men said in unison, and they

got busy with their assigned tasks. Imri began collecting the electronics while Camilo started to release Gregario from the table. Victoria and Camilo worked together to sling Gregario's arms around their shoulders and begin dragging him back through the factory.

Gregario's toes dragged as the team lugged his mostly limp body. He was still extremely wasted and didn't have the capacity to fight them. He had no idea what was going on, so he did not feel a need to resist. As they hauled him back to the utility room, Camilo asked about Robby.

"How did he look? I mean honestly," inquired Camilo.

"Well, under the circumstances, mostly good." She knew she couldn't lie to him; it would only come back to bite her in the ass. "He has a busted lip and now a small cut on his left eye. They drugged him, I'm not sure with what, but he should not feel much pain."

"He was too good of a student to do much partying," replied Camilo. "He never had any medical procedures that required anesthesia either. As far as I know, this is his first time being high."

"The biggest issue is that he is scared,"

continued Victoria. "As you know, he was not trained for this. I really screwed up getting him into this situation. I knew there was a risk, but I never imagined he would be taken like this. I am still trying to figure out how Leo made the connection."

"Yeah," agreed Camilo. "You fucked up big time on this one! Now you need to make it right. You can't let your hatred for Gregario jeopardize Robby anymore."

"I promise to do everything in my power to get him back with as little damage as possible," said Victoria earnestly. "Do you feel confident about your team?"

"I have worked closely with each of them in the past," answered Camilo. "They will hold their own. And yours?"

"Umm... I'm workin' on it," replied Vic sheepishly."

Camilo stopped. "Girl, I know you're a badass, but you'd be stupid to go at this solo."

Losing Camilo's effort, Victoria stopped dragging Gregario and turned to look at Camilo.

"I am going to get Robby back," Victoria's voice expressed determination and her face looked resolute. "I'm not fully convinced a team won't just slow me down."

Camilo got the message and felt it was best to just get back to work. He began the pull on Gregario and Victoria followed. They dragged the man the rest of the way back to the utility room in silence.

Just as they finished restraining him, Imri opened the door. He approached Gregario with his syringe kit in hand. "I thought we should give him the GHB."

"Let's keep him sedated through the flight, too," replied Vic "I don't want any issues."

"No problem." Imri nodded and pulled an additional vile from his pocket. With a slight grin, he added, "I had a feeling you might say that."

"Did I ever tell you about my friend Tamar? He got run over by a tank?" Imri tried to lighten the mood with a joke. He waited for what seemed like an eternity, but neither Victoria nor Camilo took the bait.

"Now he goes by, Crunchy," he said bursting into laughter. Imri had a slightly twisted sense of humor and would often find the oddest things amusing.

The joke was just dumb enough to work. Both Victoria and Camilo let out a slight chuckle. Not so much at the joke, but more because Imri was so amused with himself. As a result, Imri got tickled and his leg twitched slamming into Gregario's chair. He winced in pain and let out a loud "Fuuuccckkk!"

It was like a toddler watching their parent step on a Lego. You can't help but laugh at the expression of pain. Victoria and Camilo lost control and busted into laughter at Imri's expression. It didn't matter, seeing them lighten up for a second was enough encouragement for Imri to look for additional opportunities to soften them up and get them to relax a bit. Something will snap, if not. This team is spun way too tight at the moment.

After a few minutes, Vic regained her composure and jumped back into productive mode. "Let's get it all packed up and get out of here." The guys nodded and they all headed to the office to get everything prepared for the travel. They would have time on the flight during takeoff to relax for a minute before they planned the next evolution.

CHAPTER 6
DARTS, SPIES, AND CHICKEN

It only took about fifteen minutes to clean up the safehouse and remove the evidence of what had happened there. They bleached the floors and work surfaces and bagged up all the rags and trash. They would dispose of the evidence elsewhere. It took another five minutes to gather all the equipment and get it packed for transport.

As the boys loaded the gear in the van, Victoria made her call to The Skipper to ask about reinforcements.

"Hey lady," The Skipper answered.

"Hi Skipper," replied Victoria. She never addressed him properly unless it was something serious.

"What's up, girl," he asked.

"I need your help again," she said.

"Of course, you never call to chit-chat anymore." The Skipper teased her.

"The CAC's got Robby," Vic's tone was serious. "We have a trade setup, but I need some backup."

"I follow," The Skipper acknowledged the seriousness of the situation. "I assume you want me to help you find someone?"

"Exactly," replied Vic. "We lost Mark on the last op and Imri took one in the leg. I need someone who can help me handle the exchange. Someone I trust and who has what it takes to pull this off."

"I think I know where you are going with this," said The Skipper with a hint of dread in his voice.

"Yeah, I know it's a lot to ask," continued Victoria, "and I wouldn't if I had another way. Time is short and I am out of people I trust to have my six."

"What about Jimmy?" suggested The Skipper. "Or Pablo, or Smitty?"

Vic expected him to object and hoped he would think of someone suitable for the task, but as expected he did not.

"Do you really think any of them are good options? Jimmy is under surveillance from the job in Guadalajara a few months back. I can't afford any attention. Pablo hooked up with that German woman and put on about 75 pounds in the past year. He couldn't keep up. And Smitty? Are you kidding me? He doesn't follow orders from those he respects, and respecting me? Let's just say he hasn't gotten over me shooting him down when trying to get into my pants."

"Okay, okay," agreed The Skipper, "you're right, they aren't the best options."

"So will you ask him?" Victoria pleaded.

"The only way I can ask is face-to-face. How soon do you need Gordo and where?" he asked.

"The swap is the day after tomorrow," Vic answered. "I need him in Costa Rica immediately. We will be wheels up in twenty-five minutes and arriving in Costa Rica in about 12 hours."

"I'll do my best," said The Skipper. "I am floating off the coast about 200 miles south of his place so I'll see how fast I can get there in my little dingy."

The Skipper loved referring to his superyacht as a dingy. Since his boat, "World is Not Enough," is capable of 70 knots he should get there in less than three hours.

"I'll make sure Ivan has a helicopter on

standby to pick him up," said Vic. Once you convince him to help, have him work with Ivan on logistics."

"You sure do have a lot of faith in my ability to convince him," replied The Skipper.

"Even after everything, I'm pretty sure he still owes you," encouraged Vic. "He would be stuck in a cubical if you had not saved him from the shirt and tie life. Not to mention, you are the one who introduced him to Rosa."

"I'll see what I can do," said The Skipper. "But this time, you will really owe me, and I will be collecting. Perhaps I'll have you arrange another cruise with your friends Ashley and Jenifer."

"Just get it done and we can discuss the compensation later," replied Victoria with a hint of disgust in her voice.

Now that The Skipper was working on getting Gordo on board, Vic set her mind to the tasks at hand. Time to head to the airstrip and head west.

GORDO WAS one of the CIA's top operatives until he discovered he was being used to eliminate targets that had dirt on the President's Chief of Staff. The targets were innocent civilians who witnessed the

Chief of Staff accepting bribes from large foreign industrial chemical companies in exchange for U.S. government contracts. These companies were some of the highest polluters in the world and Gordo had a bit of a soft spot for his planet. Innocent people and a healthy planet were two things he felt were worth protecting.

Gordo was a bit of a legend. He was very covert and was known mostly for his achievements rather than anything personal. Those that never met him assumed he got his nickname for being overweight, or at least a very large man. But the truth is that he is average size and built more like a men's health model. Those that really knew him understood the name was simply a shorter version of his real name, Gordon Hostetler.

Gordon was an Ivy League yuppy and was the "stroke" for the Cornell University rowing team. After graduating summa cum laude, he was set to join his chemical engineering peers at Westlake Chemical, that is until he met The Skipper at a bar in Houston.

Drunk as usual, The Skipper backed into him at the bar, spilling Gordon's single malt all over his suit jacket. The Skipper, never one to admit fault, offered to pay for the cleaning if he could beat him at a game of darts. Gordon upped the ante and suggested the winner buys drinks for the night. The Skipper rarely backs down from a challenge and free drinks sounded like a great opportunity.

Gordon won every round including the one when The Skipper cheated by paying the waitress to pinch his ass just as he released the dart. Impressed by his aim, concentration, and intelligent conversation, The Skipper conceded to cover the tab on the condition that he would join him the following day at the shooting range. Gordon had never fired a weapon before but was intrigued by the invitation, so he agreed.

At the range, Gordon continued to impress The Skipper when he was able to land all of his shots in a three-inch cluster at 50 feet with The Skipper's Sig Sauer P228. After the range, the pair returned to the bar where Gordon shared stories of his adventurous side. The Skipper, who was a CIA Operation Supervisor at the time, used his skills of persuasion to convince Gordon to join The Company.

Gordon excelled at "The Farm" and was top of his training class. Not only was he an expert shot, but his intelligence and reserved demeanor made it easy for him to blend in and go unnoticed. He learned a new language to a conversational level each year and could communicate freely around the globe.

Fairly early in his career, Victoria and Gordo were chasing down the same target. Fortunately, they had a common ally in The Skipper. He was able to get them to work together to hunt down their man. They agreed that Vic would be able to interrogate the man about Gregario before Gordo took him into custody. It was a win-win for both Vic and Gordo. They learned a lot about each other during the op, they gained trust and confidence in each other. A bond was formed that she has felt with few other operators.

Years later during an op with The Skipper, Gordo spent a week surveying an asset and gathering intel in Honduras. The Skipper took Gordo to his favorite dirty alley restaurant with chickens running between the tables. They ordered the special, "Arroz con Pollo". Shortly after the waitress took their order, the sounds of a chicken being slaughtered could be heard. It was the most satiating food Gordo had ever eaten and he couldn't stop singing its praises.

The Skipper eventually tired of his yapping and took him by the arm back to the kitchen.

When Gordo stepped into the kitchen, his eyes fell on the tiny young woman in the corner cleaning off the counter for the next recipe.

"This is Rosa," said The Skipper. "She's the one that made that chicken you can't shut up about." He turned his head to look out the back door. "And from the looks of it, she just plucked it."

Rosa was mesmerized by Gordon's sweet smile and bright blue eyes. It was love at first sight, and Gordo knew he never would have found her if not for The Skipper's lunch cravings. Gordo spent all his off-op time at the restaurant, talking to her between customers. It wasn't long before the two were married.

Several years later, after discovering the Chief of Staff's indiscretions and leaving the CIA, Gordo took Rosa and disappeared off the grid into the jungle in Central America. He had a Computer Science buddy from his rowing team at Cornell erase their online existence. The only person he kept contact with was The Skipper, that is until they had their blowout.

No one really knows what their issue is. Vic tried to pry it out of The Skipper, but he refuses to talk about it. And since The Skipper is the only one who knows how to contact Gordo, no one has had an opportunity to ask him about it. Perhaps if The Skipper is able to convince him to join Victoria, she will see if Gordon will open up to her and tell her what happened.

Just as the van starts to pull out of the factory, a Barcelona Police patrol car rounded the corner of the building to the east.

"How we playin' this?" Asked Camilo from the driver's seat.

"We don't have time for delays," answered Vic. "And if they search the van, they will definitely take us in for questioning."

"Lose them," replied Camilo. "Got, it!"

He floored the gas and the tires shot rocks into the empty factory. The back of the van swung out into the road as the tires searched for traction. Imri and Victoria reached for places to hold on and brace themselves as the van took off. Gregario was unconscious, so his head just swung back and forth with every turn.

The officers were simply patrolling the area, they weren't expecting to find a van fleeing the area. Their response time was slow, giving Camilo a chance to get a jump on them before they switched on their lights and began pursuit. The howls of the siren echoed off the tall metal walls of the factories as it sped after the van. The race was on!

"Try to head in the direction of the airport," instructed Vic. "The plane is waiting."

"Workin' on it," Camilo hollered back as he threw the steering wheel to the left, and the passengers on the right were slammed against the side of the van.

Camilo used the short quick turns to avoid straightaways where the police car could close the gap. Being an excellent driver, he knew how to control the van through the maze of factories. The team was able to get out of the industrial district with a ten-second lead. Camilo slammed the gas pedal to the floor and the van picked up speed as he merged onto the main road. He dodged a sedan on his left and squeezed along the guard rail passing cars and searching for an opening.

A motorcyclist swerved and slammed on his brakes as Camilo cut him off, forcing his way into the lane. Another strong acceleration and Camilo increased their lead, thanks to the congestion of traffic blocking the patrol car. He passed a semi-truck and a minivan before crossing two lanes to make a right turn. The patrol car was far enough back to make the lane change and take the turn in pursuit.

It was clear that Camilo was a superior driver to the patrol officer. There is no reason the patrol car should not have overtaken the van. It was simply a matter of a rookie driver against a seasoned veteran.

When they were close to the airport, Camilo knew he would need to make a move. He took another hard right and ducked into an alley where he pulled in behind a beer truck with its doors open, making a delivery. The team held their breath as they counted the seconds. A few moments later the siren blared by as they watched the lights race across the driver's door mirror. The cops didn't see them and passed the turn. Camilo hit the gas again and looped back toward the airstrip.

"Which side of the airport is the plane on?" he asked.

"The south runway," Vic answered.

"Tell them to fire up the engines," he ordered.

Vic grabbed her phone and called Ivan. "We're coming in hot!" she said abruptly into the phone.

"Tell them to start the engines, we need to take off immediately!"

He must have taken the instruction and known not to ask questions because she hung up and slammed the phone back into her pocket.

With no sign of the police, they rounded the south side of the airport. Camilo spotted a soft spot in the fence and decided to take the shortest route to the plane. They drove straight through, and the section of chain link ripped from the posts and scraped across the top of the van. Camilo pulled up alongside the plane and the team sprang into action unloading the van and boarding the plane.

They slammed the door behind them, and the pilot pulled back on the throttle. The plane lurched into taxi and they were in the air before the police were able to track them to the airport.

CHAPTER 7

FINE LEATHER, JET EXHAUST, AND GUN OIL

T he plane climbed through the overcast sky and the team all looked at each other and chuckled.

"Just another Tuesday, huh boys?" Vic joked.

"Wouldn't have it any other way," said Imri who seemed to be enjoying the excitement of the day.

"Great driving, brother," he added.

"Thanks," replied Camilo with an expression of pride augmenting his grin.

"Take a few to relax," instructed Vic. "We will be briefing the mission with Ivan and Priya in a bit so take some time to clear your heads."

"Roger that," acknowledged Imri.

Camilo gave a nod and laid his head back against the headrest.

The smell of fine leather mixed with the jet exhaust created a feeling of class. Victoria felt a bit guilty relaxing in the luxurious aircraft. Since they arrived at the safe house, she had not had a shower. They were only able to sponge off in the sink and she was feeling a bit like a homeless person. Her dingy clothes were a stark contrast to the fine upholstery of the Gulfstream G700.

Speeding across the sky, she looked to the forward seating area where they had strapped in Gregario. His head rested against the wall as he sat unconscious. Anger and frustration climbed as she considered what he had said during the interrogation. It was clear he was not remorseful in the least. The thought of having to let him go was a bitter pill to swallow.

Her mind raced for any course of action that would include recovering Robby without releasing Gregario. It was obvious that Camilo was not open to any plan that jeopardized the recovery of Robby or put him further in harm's way. If she could come up with a way to accomplish his return and still hold on to Gregario, she would have to be very cautious and choose her words wisely when presenting it to Camilo.

Since it would be hours before the briefing, Victoria headed back to try to rest. Camilo had already taken up residence on the couch in the entertainment area and Imri was curled up on the sofa in the galley. Their experience had taught them to find comfort and rest when time allowed. Laying back on the plush mattress, she closed her eyes and drifted off to sleep, but not for long.

A buzz on Victoria's watch stirred her from sleep. She had mastered the art of power napping. Her body had learned how to get the maximum benefit from minimum sleep. She sat up feeling quite refreshed and ready to focus. It had been four hours since she had talked to The Skipper. The display on the watch was a contact request from Ivan.

Walking through the cabin, Victoria nudged Imri and Camilo to wake them. "Ivan's got news; time for the briefing."

Getting set up in the entertainment area, Vic used the remote to raise the hidden monitor complete with a webcam from the side panel. It flickered on and displayed the options for entertainment or the web. Selecting the web option, she quickly logged into the plane's Wi-Fi and established a secure connection. Ivan appeared on the screen with Deadpool mug in hand.

"Hello Ivan," said Vic as she brushed her bangs behind her right ear.

Camilo arrived with a round of Auchentoshan Three Wood Scotch from the bar in the galley. "I thought these might help. I have a feeling we are going to need them."

Handing one to Victoria, he and Imri took the seats on either side of her on the couch. The monitor split as Priya's connection was added. With the team all there, Ivan began to organize the briefing.

"Good to see you all. First things first, let's go over our team," started Ivan. The screen flashed to display an org chart.

"Obviously, Priya and I will be handling intel, tech, and logistics. Imri, Vic said that because of your leg injury, you will be on overwatch. That brings us to the tactical teams."

On the monitor, Ivan displayed Camilo and two other images. "Camilo's team will include Eduardo "Guayo" Solano and Joseph "Chepe"

Garcia, both of who served with Camilo in the Unidad Especial de Intervención (UEI). Guayo is an ordnance specialist and small arms expert. Chepe excels at hand-to-hand combat and marksmen skills."

Another flash and the images were replaced with Victoria and a man that resembled Benedict Cumberbatch. "Vic's team will include herself and Gordon "Gordo" Hostetler. Gordo is an ex-CIA covert operative. In addition to his impeccable aim, his intelligence is near genius level."

"Are you talking about "Gordo" that recovered the documents about chemical weapons plants in Libya and took out Khalid something, the head of that terrorist group?" Ivan asked, impressed by Vic's choice.

"That's him," answered Victoria. "I did an op with him shortly after he became a special agent before he built his reputation."

"So, I guess The Skipper was able to pull it off," said Victoria.

The monitor transitioned back to Ivan and Priya.

"Well..." Ivan hesitated sheepishly. "The Skipper said that Gordo said he'll do it, but you are going to owe him one and he was planning on collecting."

"What did he mean by "owe him one"," asked Vic.

"I don't know, he wouldn't say," replied Ivan. "I was hoping you might know."

"I guess I will have to deal with that later," said Vic. "I really need his help now."

"So, what's the plan?" asked Camilo. "I hope you aren't considering doing something stupid, like getting Robby killed."

"I can't lie," said Vic. "I have searched my brain for a way to not have to give up Gregario."

"I knew it!" yelled Camilo. "You selfish bitch, you would rather get your revenge than save Robby's life."

"Wait a minute," Imri interjected, trying to keep the peace. "She was trying to be honest, and you can't blame her for wanting everything. Besides, she said she was thinking, not planning."

"I haven't been able to find a way," Vic began her defense. "Robby's safety is the priority, but I have been hunting Gregario for over a decade and I finally have him. I would be lying if I said it wasn't hard to let him go after all I've been through to get here. And yes, if I could get Robby back and keep Gregario I would. So, I will continue to look for opportunities to get everything. But saving Robby comes first."

"There is no risk worth Robby," Camilo was clear in his position. If Vic did come up with a plan, he would not be willing to hear it until Robby was safe in his custody.

Sensing it was a good time to try to shift the subject, Priya spoke up. "I have been tracking the movements of some of the known members of the CAC. Some have been flying into the San Jose airport in Costa Rica and others are landing at the Enrique Malek International Airport in northern Panama."

Priya took over the screen and displayed a map of Costa Rica and Panama that showed the two airports.

The map zoomed in on the Osa Peninsula and a marker was placed on the southern tip near Playa Pan Dulce. Then it split to show a photo of a young man holding flippers, a spear gun, and some fish.

"Do you recognize this person?" asked Priya. "This is one of the few photos my software was able to link to the man who has Robby. I ran the video through my recognition software, and it linked the face to this photo of Leo that was posted on a blog by a tourist years ago. I then ran a search for the background, and it came up with the location for "Casa Bamboo", an off-the-grid cabina available for rent. It is a rustic place with open air shutters without screens, limited solar power, mosquito nets over the bed, and one Wifi router with only 25mbps service."

Priya wrapped up her presentation, "Based on this intel, I believe the swap will be taking place in southern Costa Rica, perhaps on the Osa Peninsula."

"Good work, Priya!" encouraged Victoria. "This is what I'm talking about, we need to get ahead of them so we can be proactive, not reactive. I need the two of you to keep an eye on the area and try to get as much intel as possible as to what type of force we will be facing."

"I have been capturing and analyzing satellite footage," added Ivan. "So far there are four men at Casa Bamboo. One of the men is on roaming patrol at all times. The others spend most of the time indoors."

The screen swapped images to a satellite view

of the property with an infrared overlay. The heat signatures of the guard and the men in the building were clearly visible.

"Perfect," said Vic. "Let us know if more show up or if you have any other developments. And send me the coordinates so I can establish our plan."

"Of course," replied Ivan.

The screen transitioned back to Ivan and Priya's cameras.

"Where will we rendezvous with the other team members?" asked Camilo.

Priya spoke up since she was handling travel logistics. "Gordo, Chepe, and Guayo will meet you both at the San Jose airport. I have a helicopter standing by to take you to the swap location once you confirm it with Leo."

"Ask The Skipper if he can hang out in the area," instructed Vic. "I think we may need separate approach points. Based on the location you sent, there are a lot of trees that may prevent a clean line of sight for Imri. The best place for long-range cover may be from the water off the coast."

"Are you boys up for a jump?" Vic looked for confirmation from Camilo and especially Imri.

With his leg injury, she needed to know he felt he could handle the impact of a parachute landing.

"I've never jumped from a jet like this. If it's a big enough clearing I should be good." Imri confirmed with a bit of enthusiasm. A large area would allow him to make a shallower approach minimizing the force of the impact.

"I'm good for a jump," added Camilo.

"Based on our recent encounters with Leo," continued Vic, "There's a good chance he'll be watching us from the moment we land. I will take Gordo and Gregario with me in the helicopter from the airport. Have Guayo and Chepe wait for Camilo and Imri on The Skipper's yacht. You boys can make a water landing which should be a softer impact for Imri. Camilo, I think it might be best for your team to make a beach approach. Are your boys good for a swim?"

"They are expert frogmen," answered Camilo. "I'm sure they are up for it."

"Priya, have a helicopter on standby in case the exchange isn't where we expect," instructed Vic. "Camilo's team and Imri may need a lift to the location of the swap if we are wrong."

"I'll have one ready," agreed Priya.

"We have about ten hours until we land. Guys

get some rest and prepare for the op. Ivan and Priya, send us updates on new intel." Victoria closed out the meeting and the screen receded back into the cabinet.

Vic headed to the cargo hold to grab her laptop and weapons. Victoria found great relaxation in breaking down and cleaning her weapons. She also wanted to spend some time researching the area to help finalize their plans. She placed her equipment on the table in the dining area.

Hearing the click of the rear pin and slide of the charging handle of her BCM Recce AR, Imri and Camilo's heads popped out into the passageway. Seeing that Vic was setting up to clean her weapons, the men decided to retrieve their own and join her in the cleaning session.

Victoria connected her phone to the plane's entertainment system and started her playlist titled "Instrumental Metal." The sound of shredding guitars and the rhythmic booms of the drums drowned out most of the wind noise of the jet. The team did not speak but their heads bobbed to the beat as they cleaned and lubricated their arsenals.

Relaxed and with their tools ready for the coming tasks, the men retired to their perspective couches for more rest. Victoria opened up her laptop and began her research on the Osa Peninsula. She had visited the peninsula as a teenager with her cousin Richie and had surfed Playa Pan Dulce, the beach near the cabina. It had been many years, but she recalled the magic of this wild and secluded little piece of the world.

CHAPTER 8
THE PLUNGE

Tumbling through the wash of the wave, Victoria could hear the low-toned guttural roar of humpback whales. At first, it was quite frightening as it sounded as though they were right behind her; but in reality, they were about 500 meters away. The water carries low tones with amazing clarity for long distances. Her head breached the surface to hear Richie's laughter.

"You really ate it hard on that one," he said between chuckles. "I bet you drank a bucket full, didn't you?"

"Yeah," replied Victoria. "But I am pretty sure I peed it out when I heard the whale."

"It's amazing how loud they are, isn't it?" Richie asked as he sat on his board looking back over his shoulder at the next set rolling in.

Just as Richie popped up onto a beautifully cresting wave, Victoria was pulled from her dream back to reality. She could hear the men talking toward the front of the plane. She grabbed her hash pen and took a few drags as she headed to the front to see what was up.

Imri was administering another dose to Gregario, ensuring he would not wake before they landed. As he finished, he began to hand his injection kit to Victoria.

"He is going to need another dose in about four hours," he instructed. "You will need to dose him every four hours until you are ready for him to regain consciousness. If you want him loopy but conscious, use the vials with the red stripes and fill the syringe the same. The timing is the same, every four hours."

"We are about an hour from the drop zone," said Camilo. "We will need to get everything in the baggage compartment strapped down and move any loose items to the main cabin."

Vic nodded in agreement and turned to head back to the baggage compartment to get started.

The men followed. It only took about five minutes to secure the gear and remove the small items, especially since the parachutes and the guys' gear were a large part of the baggage.

The three of them headed back to the entertainment area for a last-minute status check with Ivan and to relax for a few before they put on their chutes and strapped on their gear. Ivan reported a few new arrivals to the Casa Bamboo house and confirmed that the other team members had made it to their respective rendezvous points where they were waiting for Imri, Camilo, and Victoria to arrive.

"As usual, The Skipper is excited to help out and is looking forward to a little action, even if it is from afar," said Ivan. "He offered to help Imri with overwatch as a spotter and potential second shooter. He said he is just hoping they can stay far enough out that his "little dingy" won't take any hits."

"I am assuming we have not heard anything new from Leo?" asked Victoria.

"No," answered Ivan. "The instructions are still for you and Gregario to go to the resort and wait for coordinates and instructions."

"We'll be at the airport ready to board the helicopter in about an hour and fifteen minutes," said Vic. "Tell Gordo I am going to need some help dragging this piece of shit to the chopper."

"You got it, Vic," acknowledged Imri.

They signed off and the men began donning their parachutes and gear.

"I gotta' tell ya, buddy," began Imri excitedly. "It's been a while since I made a jump. And I can't remember the last time I made a water landing."

"Yeah," agreed Camilo. "It's been a long time for me too, but I too am excited to take the plunge! I have never jumped out of anything this nice before, it's usually a cargo plane."

Vic was glad to see the men relaxed and excited about the mission or at least the rendezvous plan. Camilo's excitement distracted him from his anger toward Victoria for putting Robby in danger. Hopefully, this positive vibe would continue for a while.

The plane banked as it rounded the Panama Canal and lined up for the drop. The Skipper was floating off the top of the peninsula far enough from the assumed swap point to avoid being noticed. Once Imri and Camilo were on board, they would sail down the coast and around the tip to where they could make some passes by the location and get some visual intel. From there they would look for the optimal insertion point for Camilo's team.

The G700 slowed and decreased altitude to 14,000 feet to try to minimize the risk of the jump. Although the jet was not designed for skydiving, it is a luxury jet after all, and not many high rollers decide to hop out mid-flight, it was equipped with the most sophisticated instrumentation and high-end equipment allowing for unintended uses.

"We're on approach," the captain said over the intercom. "We'll be over the drop site in three minutes."

Vic gave Imri and Camilo high fives as they loaded into the cargo hold. "Enjoy the ride boys," said Vic with a nod. "Can't say I'm not a little jealous of your transportation arrangements."

"Yeah," agreed Imri with a big grin. "We definitely got the better deal on this one."

Vic closed the interior door to the cargo hold and a moment later the captain lowered the exterior door and stairs.

"We're over the drop zone," the captain reported over the intercom. "You have a 30-second window to drop."

The men walked down the steps backward and

Camilo stepped off the last step and was sucked out into the clear blue sky. Imri followed not more than five seconds behind, and they both began their free fall for the ocean below.

As soon as the jumpers were clear, the pilot raised the stairs and closed the cargo hatch. The plane climbed to a cruising altitude of 30,000 feet and the pilot banked the plane back toward the San Jose airport. Victoria took a seat across the aisle from Gregario and stared at the face of the man she had been hunting for over a decade. She spent the rest of the flight searching for a way to finish him without putting any more risk on Robby.

The free fallers could see the coastline in the distance and a tiny dot on the water that was "The World Is Not Enough." From this altitude, The Skipper's superyacht looked like a canoe. Feeling frisky and enjoying the rush, Camilo pulled in his arms and bulleted toward the surface. Not wanting to be left out of the fun Imri followed suit for a moment before considering that increased speed was probably not the best idea for a soft landing. He needed to make sure he didn't land too hard on his injured leg, so he pulled his arms back out and slowed his descent allowing Camilo to race ahead.

Diving faster and faster, Camilo stiffened his cheeks as the cool humid air blew across his face. He felt adrenaline-charged on the edge of control and the speed was incredibly exhilarating. The wind whistled through the gear strapped to his body. His heart pounded in his ears drowning out some of the wind noise as he took in the moment. Time slowed as he raced toward the rich blue ocean.

After fifteen seconds, Camilo had enough, slowed his descent, and resumed freefall posture. The drop put him considerably closer to the ground allowing more time between him and Imri hitting the water. Not only was it an amazing rush, but he would be picked up first so he could help get Imri and his gear out of the water quickly.

With the yacht clearly in sight, Camilo was perfectly lined up to land just off its starboard side. Pulling his canopy, his body swings upright and he takes a look around. The sun is bright and pierces the surface of the water.

Looking down to his left, Camilo spots a large humpback breaching the surface. It is migration season in the area and the humpbacks are plentiful. The massive sea beast creates a colossal splash as it slaps down sideways on the water. Eyeing across the water, he is able to see many of the gigantic creatures just below the surface.

Camilo spots his landing and maneuvers for contact. He wants to be close enough not to have to swim far but doesn't want to misjudge his landing and slam into the side of the yacht. One last adjustment and he drops in fifteen meters from the back of the boat. The gear is heavy, and he has to work hard to swim to the stern of the boat. As he climbs the ladder out of the water, crewmen grab his arms and help him aboard.

He quickly unstraps his equipment and drops his harness. Camilo watches Imri as he approaches from the rear of the Yacht. Once all of his gear is off, he joins the crewmen on the platform ready to fish Imri out of the water.

Pulling hard on the lines of the chute, Imri lifts his boots as he slides gently through the surface of the sea. The 80° water feels amazing and his face exhibits pure joy. Imri is only ten meters from the yacht and one of the crewmen readies a pole to reach out toward him. Camilo grabs the life ring and throws it out for Imri to grab. Once Imri's arm is wrapped around the ring, Camilo begins dragging him to the boat ladder.

"Fucking AMAZING!" yells Imri from the water.

"Amazing indeed!" agrees Camilo. "Did you see all those whales?"

"I must have counted twenty of them on the way down," Ivan said excitedly.

Camilo helped Imri off with his gear and the pair looked up to be greeted by The Skipper who was looking down from the main deck.

"Welcome aboard," he hollered, lifting a beer in a toast. "Come get a cold one."

Camilo and Imri made their way to the aft deck entertainment area. Reaching the top of the stairs, Camilo spots a couple of familiar faces. Sitting back in the deck chairs with drinks in hand are Chepe and Guayo. They raise their drinks with a unison chorus of "Hey!"

Camilo greets each of them with a handshake hug, just the kind of reunion you might expect from warriors. In their pink and yellow polo shirts and flip-flops, Chepe and Guayo look like a couple of tourists visiting for a fishing trip. They do not look a bit threatening, perhaps not even to the fish. The scene just looks like a bunch of buddies reunited to get drunk, tell stories, and forget about home.

A crewman came to take Camilo and Imri's drink orders and the two sat down with Chepe and Guayo to relax.

"At this point, we are just waiting to hear from Vic," The Skipper announced. "Until she gets further instruction we are to just hang out and wait. I have instructed my crew to stow your gear in your staterooms. Enjoy my "little dingy" and let my crewmen know if you need anything."

With his announcement complete,The Skipper raised his glass, "Cheers."

Everyone joined the toast and settled in for a relaxing afternoon. Under the shade of the helm deck, the ocean breeze cooled the humid tropical air as they gently sailed along the coast. The crew stayed busy bringing drinks and hors d'oeuvres.

"Boy, Vic really did get the short end of the stick," Imri said as he sipped his Scotch.

"Yeah, I was excited about the jump," agreed Camilo. "But I hadn't considered the rest of the day. She's probably just arrived at the airport and still has to take a chopper to the resort."

"I expect we won't hear from her for several hours," added The Skipper.

The conversation returned to war stories and lies about exotic women. The men had a great time unwinding and catching up. The perfect weather and luxury of the yacht created an unbeatable relaxing setting. It was exactly what they needed before the mission ahead.

CHAPTER 9
I KNOW WE WILL TAKE FIRE

The glare of the early morning sun moved to allow Victoria's eyes to catch sight of Gordo standing by a helicopter. It had been years since she had seen him, and she had forgotten how captivating he was. There was no real romantic attraction with Gordo, but man, he was fun to look at.

The sleeves of his button-down t-shirt fit snugly around his muscular arms. He pulled down his sunglasses for a better look, revealing his beautiful blue eyes. The edges of his mouth turned up to a kind grin and Victoria's mind took a snapshot.

Gordo offered a smile and a wave, then stepped forward to offer his assistance.

"I hear you need a little help," Gordo greeted.

"Yes, I do," answered Victoria. "It's great to see you Gordo."

"Good to see you too, Victoria," replied Gordo.

"Come help me transport this asshole," Vic suggested.

"Lead the way," agreed Gordo, and he followed her back into the plane.

The pair worked together to transfer Gregario and Vic's gear to the helicopter. Once everything and everyone was loaded, the chopper took to the skies, and before long, they were flying over volcanoes. Soaring over the canopy, they flew together with several species of birds. The tropical terrain whizzed by under them and Victoria took in the beauty of the rainforest from above.

The helicopter set down on the grassy area near the entrance of the resort. Ivan had hacked Robby's email and sent a message about some special guests. The message instructed them to assign rooms for Vic and Gordo away from other visitors and to meet the helicopter with a wheelchair for a disabled guest. As the helicopter's rotor stopped, the resort worker approached with the wheelchair.

Again, Victoria and Gordo worked together to

transfer Gregario and their gear from the helicopter to their rooms.

With the last bag in hand, Victoria turned to Gordo and said, "I'm going to get cleaned up. Assuming I don't get a call before then, let's meet in about an hour to brief."

"Sounds like a plan," agreed Gordo. "I'm going to freshen up myself and maybe check out the resort. Give me a call when you're ready."

Victoria dropped the bag against the wall and grabbed her things to shower. It had been almost a week since she'd had a shower, and the factory was filthy. She tried to clean up in the sink when she could, but there is only so much you can do without a shower.

Letting the hot water pour over her head, she felt the grime slide away and she imagined herself like a butterfly coming out of a cocoon. Vic may be a tough operator, but her alter ego Victoria liked to feel beautiful and it's hard to feel beautiful if no one can see through your dirt crust.

Fresh from the shower and with a clean outfit, Vic searched the resort for a girl named Sonya whom Robby had introduced her to on her last visit. Sonya worked in the spa area and was very talented and fast at braiding hair. After spending the last week trying to pull her long hair up to keep it out of the way, it was time for a longer-lasting solution. She just hoped Sonya had come in early to set up the spa for the day.

She was in luck, and with a little persuasion, Sonya agreed to take care of Victoria's hair before finishing her spa tasks. Sonya was working on the last braid when Vic sent a message to Gordo asking him to meet her at the restaurant. When Sonya finished, Victoria paid her generously and thanked her for taking care of her.

To Gordo, it seemed like Victoria changed her look every time he saw her. As she walked into the bar, he had to comment on her new hairdo.

"Nice rows," he said pointing at his head with a grin. "That should keep that hair out of your eyes."

"Yeah, you like it?" Victoria said proudly. "Let's get some food and head to the room. I think it will be easier to go over everything with my laptop, and I want to be ready in case I get the call."

Back in the room, Vic pulled the injection kit from her bag and administered another dose to Gregario who was strapped to the wheelchair. With him taken care of, she sat down at the table and picked up a forkful of gallo pinto. Dipping her fried plantain in her strawberry yogurt she looked up at Gordo with a mouthful of food.

"Hungry?" Gordo teased, pointing at the yogurt dripping from the corner of her mouth.

Vic wiped her mouth with her hand and licked the yogurt off her fingers. "Yep."

"So, are you sure you can let him go?" Gordo asked, nodding in the direction of Gregario.

"I have to," replied Vic. "I have to save Robby. It's my fault he's in danger and it's my responsibility to get him out of it, no matter the cost."

"But you have been pursuing this guy so long," he said, "You were tracking him when we did that op on the Baja Peninsula. How do you just walk away?"

"It's like they say," answered Vic, "It's not "goodbye", it's "bye for now," I swear I will find him again. And when I do, I won't waste time, I'll finish the job quickly."

"So, what's the plan?" asked Gordo.

"We wait for Leo, the man who has Robby, to call and tell us where to meet. We will then go to that place and do what we can to get Robby and get out alive."

"Sounds pretty straightforward," Gordo said,

and his expression conveyed a "what could possibly go wrong" attitude.

A proud grin crept onto Vic's face. "I have a pretty awesome team I've put together." She sounded like a proud parent whose kid just got student of the year. "Camilo and Imri are two of the best operators I've worked with, present people included. My tech team has been able to get us some intel that may just be the advantage we need to pull this off."

The "Flight of the Valkyries" ringtone broke up the briefing and Victoria took a deep breath. With her thoughts focused she answered the call. "Hola..."

"Hola Victoria." Leo's voice had an effect on her that was unsettling. Something about his tone and accent stirred her.

"Where are we doing this?" Vic tried to take some control.

"No small talk, just right down to business; okay. I will message the coordinates now." Leo replied, a bit surprised by her boldness. "I expect Mr. Gregario is in good shape?"

"Yes," Vic said shortly. "He's resting comfortably."

"He will need to be conscious when he

arrives," Leo instructed. "You must be at the location in 10 hours."

"10 hours," acknowledged Vic, and the call terminated.

The alert on her phone sounded to announce the arrival of the coordinates. Vic clicked the link and the map snapped to the southern tip of the Osa Peninsula. She forwarded the coordinates to Ivan with a message that said, "Priya was right!"

Gordo sat back and admired Vic's skillfulness as she managed her situation and team. She grabbed her laptop from her backpack. Sliding some food aside to set up on the table, she nearly knocked over her glass bottle of Coca-Cola. She threw back a swig as she took her place behind the keyboard.

The connection was completed and Ivan sipped from his Deadpool mug as Vic brushed her hair behind her right ear. "Everyone is online," reported Ivan. Priya and The Skipper's cameras appeared on the screen next to his. The Skipper's camera showed all the team members on board seated around a table.

"What's the plan?" asked Camilo.

"Ivan, display the coordinates I sent you," instructed Vic.

The screen shrunk the cameras to a cluster on the right and the primary display was a map of the Osa Peninsula with a pin in the location of the coordinates. The map changed to a satellite view showing the rooftop of Casa Bamboo and the coastline. There was a small opening between the cabin and the water that was surrounded by dense trees.

"Leo said we have 10 hours to get there, that is 6 p.m." Vic began to brief the team. "He knows where Gregario and I are and that would allow us time to drive to the location. Since we have a helicopter, we can be there in one hour."

"Based on our history," Ivan interjected. "I assume he has people watching you. If you were to drive, I'm sure they'd follow. But since you are planning on taking the helicopter, I'm assuming he'll just track you on radar and satellite. I'm sure he has the capability."

"Exactly," agreed Victoria. "I have to assume he will be tracking me; the question is, does he know where the rest of you are? Was he able to locate us in Barcelona? Or track us from the factory back to Costa Rica? Let's hope he was not able to locate us until we landed in San Jose. If that's the case, he does not know that you are already there."

"I don't expect them to let us just stroll out with Robby and disappear into the sunset." Vic continued. "I know we will take fire. Why wouldn't they just take Gregario and wipe us out? So how do we get out alive? We will have to establish an escape route and pray Camilo's team can cover us and attract some of the attention off of us."

Ivan gave screen control to Vic so she could use markups.

"I need you men to take up positions here, here, and here." She began making arrows from the water to three separate spots along the beach. "If you make your insertion soon, they may not be expecting you, which makes it easier to get in undetected. You will need to remain motionless at these points for several hours, so make yourself comfortable."

The Skipper picked up a radio and instructed the helmsmen to make a course near the location. "Cruising at a speed so as not to draw attention, we will be in drop range for these little swimmers in about thirty minutes," he announced. "We made a pass a few hours ago and there is a clear line of sight through the opening of the beach to the cabina. If we are close enough, Imri and I should be able to offer some decent suppression fire from the boat should you need it."

"Perfect," said Vic excitedly. Things weren't looking terribly grim after all. "The rest of the plan is simple. Gordo and I will arrive with Gregario and will only release him when they have released Robby. Once Robby is in custody, we will make our exit and you all will provide cover."

"My team will be entering from the road to the property, and they will expect us to extract that same way. We will land the helicopter at the nearest airfield and drive to the coast. There is only one road into the area so we would most likely encounter resistance and roadblocks on the way back out. Instead, we will use the chopper for extraction."

Vic panned and zoomed in on a second clearing deeper into the forest about a kilometer. "This is our best option out. After dropping us at the airfield, I will have the pilot fly to this clearing and wait for us. Gordo and I will lead Robby along this stream to the clearing. I hiked this area with my cousin as a kid and there are several animal trails leading to the water which should provide us a fast path through the thick jungle to the clearing. Camilo's team will provide cover so we can get clear of the men near the cabina and escape into the jungle. You will then exfil back to the beach, where you will disappear into the ocean and The Skipper will fish you out."

There was little discussion over the plan. They all realized that the more basic the scheme, the better odds of it going as planned. There is no way to plan for all contingencies, so it is better to trust your skills and assume they will help you address the unexpected as it arises. They all knew the most important thing is just don't get shot. The rest will work itself out.

Vic signed off and she and Gordo spent some time catching up before they had to take the flight south. It was good to hear about his love for his wife Rosa and about their simple yet labor-intensive life off the grid in Panama. When the conversation had sufficient small talk, she decided to risk asking.

"So...what happened with The Skipper?"

CHAPTER 10
FROGMEN

The Skipper cast fishing lines into the water and instructed the helmsman to adjust the course to stay one kilometer from the shore and reduce their speed to troll. He told Chef Louis to put on a Hawaiian shirt and straw hat, grab a couple of beers, and man the poles in the water. The idea was that The Skipper and Louis would look like a couple of regular guys on a fishing excursion as they drifted by and dropped off the swimmers. At their distance from shore, it would be difficult for anyone to make out the men floating in the water as the yacht drifted away.

The swimmers would need to float as motion-less as possible until the fishing lines passed. Once clear of the hooks, they would swim to shore without creating a splash or bobbing where the motion could be noticeable from shore. Camilo's team had been trained for water insertions such as this. They were used to stealth swimming while weighted down with gear. The men were excellent swimmers who grew up surfing waters like this.

"Perfect conditions for today's evolution brothers," said Camilo as they prepared to disembark.

The sun was high in the sky with only a few cirrus clouds. The rails were hot from the sun and the warm breeze felt more like a convection oven having a cooling effect. Fortunately, the hot air temperature made the tropical water feel cooler than you would expect. It was refreshing and comfortable.

"We're entering the drop zone," announced The Skipper. "First man up, let's go."

Guayo was first to climb down the rope ladder they had rigged off the starboard side away from the shore. Imri helped him get over the rail and begin his descent. He eased into the water until he was being dragged by the rope. He looked up at Camilo who gave him a thumbs up and he let go of the ladder. Guayo's body sank into the water, leaving only his head slightly protruding from the water.

As the yacht continued its course, Guayo floated with his eyes just above the surface. His boonie hat helped disguise his head. When he needed a breath, he would gently raise up out of the water just enough to inhale without taking in water. Once his lungs filled, he would sink back down into the water.

Coming out of the shadow of the boat, Guayo eyed the coast and counted until he was sure he was clear of the fishing lines. Easing forward, he began his frog kick and started the long swim to shore. It's difficult to maintain the balance between speed and stealth; but if they were to error, it would be better to be slow and unnoticed than fast and discovered.

Fortunately, the tide was on the way in. They could simply float and ride the tide into shore, but that would take quite a while. A consistent kick would shorten the swim time considerably.

Camilo was next up to get wet. They were directly out from Casa Bamboo. If the guards were watching, they would have their best vantage at this point. Imri helped steady Camilo as he swung his leg over the side and mounted the ladder. At the bottom, he assumed the position of being dragged where he could slide into his motionless float.

"We've got you covered, my friend," Imri assured him, looking down at Camilo who nodded as he released the ladder and drifted off behind the yacht.

It wasn't more than three seconds after the boat passed that Camilo watched the fishing line about ten feet in front of him drop sharply and bounce back out of the water. He slowly turned his head toward the yacht to see the rod on the starboard holder bend sharply.

"Fish on!" yelled The Skipper at Chef Louis. Louis grabbed the pole, placed it in his belt, and began reeling. This could be a fortunate event or the worst possible thing that could happen. If the guards on the shore were in fact watching, the fish could solidify their cover of being on a fishing trip. On the other hand, if they weren't paying attention before, watching a man reel in a fish is a bit captivating. This could draw more attention, making it harder for the men in the water to remain unnoticed.

Camilo kept his eyes on the line as it swung out toward him. The fish had apparently tried to turn out away from the boat. It would be disastrous for him to get caught up in the line. He did his best to stay motionless as he watched the line drift in and out.

He reached his arm out in front of him just below the surface of the water as the line drew close. Camilo felt the line slide across his palm as he tried to keep it at a distance from his body. He was thankful he was wearing his tactical gloves. He was expecting to have to crawl across some rocks and reefs on his way to shore so he wanted to protect his hands. Now those gloves were protecting the line from slicing through his palm.

The line swung back away from him, and he pulled his knife from its sheath. If the fish pulled the line back into him, he would cut the line and avoid the potential of getting caught up in it. As he tred water, the line disappeared below the surface. Looking down, he watched the sun reflect off a long shiny fish with zebra stripes.

The fish flexed hard as it was being dragged. Camilo recognized it from his young days fishing with his father. The wahoo was about a meter-and-a-half long and had beautiful markings. It would be a great catch for Louis, and he was thankful he did not have to cut it loose.

Clear of the hooks, Camilo began his swim to shore. "The World is not Enough" continued its course along the shoreline. Chepe hung at the end of the ladder looking up at Imri. Louis swapped sides of the stern to pull the fish more to the port side. Imri waited until Louis took up position on the port side to give the sign to drop. Chepe released the rope and once clear of the fish and hooks, joined the other two on approach to their respective positions.

The water felt amazing, and the swim was relatively easy. A leatherback turtle surfaced to take a breath and get a better look at Chepe as he gently kicked toward the shore. The men rode the tide with as little movement above the surface as possible, taking in the beauty of the ocean while keeping an eye on the shore.

As the beach grew near, Camilo hid behind a rock outcropping. He surveyed the beach and tree line to check if anyone was watching. There were no guards that he could see stationed on the beach. The only one he spotted was walking the small cliff path near the cabina on roaming patrol.

On the side nearest him, there was a dense tree line that could provide cover if he could get across the beach unseen. With the tide near its peak, the beach was fairly short, only about twenty-five meters. The problem was that there was a shallow rock shelf about fifty meters long that he would have to swim/crawl across to get to the sand.

Since the guard had just passed, Camilo assumed this was as good a time as any to breach the shore. He gently pushed off the rock and floated for the shelf. On the shelf, his body would be visible through the water. This is where it would be most important to be fast.

Camilo's fingers reached around the edges of the rock in front of him, and pulling hard with his arms, he propelled forward across the shelf. The gloves protected him from the sea anemones and jagged edges of the rock. As he placed his hands, crabs and starfish would scatter. The waves pushed him forward and his vest dragged on the rock in spots.

The water shallowed and he began to bear-crawl. A few meters later, he rose to his feet and made the sprint for the trees. The unstable stones got smaller and turned to sand under his boots as he ran. He spotted where he would breach the cover of the trees and foliage and ducked out of site.

Chepe was next to make landfall. Because he

was further south along the shore, they did not expect any guards to be watching or patrolling this far out. However, anyone spotting a man emerging from the water with weapons would raise alarm and give away the element of surprise, so he needed to remain unseen.

His landing spot did not have a rock shelf, but rather a sandy beach. The beach was steep and dropped off quickly in the water. Chepe drifted in unnoticed and bear-crawled his way into the ferns beneath a group of palm trees.

To the north, Guayo was trying not to drift too close to a group of surfers. This surf spot was amazing! The sets would come in threes and the locals had worked out the rotation of who caught the first wave, the second, and the third. The first surfer would pop up and a moment later there was one right behind him, and then one behind her. For the next set, they would rotate who got which wave. About one in ten would curl into a nice tube. Guayo couldn't help but imagine himself and his friends from his youth on those waves.

Fortunately, the rapid pace of the sets kept the surfers focused on the next ride. The current stayed in Guayo's favor as well, and he drifted around the corner, just out of sight of the surfers.

He quickly traversed the rock outcropping and dove into the jungle.

With all men to shore, step one was complete. Now for each man to get to their post without being discovered, each man must sneak over 200 meters to their assigned position. Along the way, they would need to pass by the guards unnoticed.

The men moved through the forest of palm trees, ferns, and huge leaf plants inland. They kept a vigilant eye for any of the cartel's men. Ivan had updated them with the latest numbers. Priya hacked a satellite feed to identify any humans on the property. They spotted a total of twelve men. Most of the men stayed in the bamboo structure, but four remained on patrol. Every four hours they would rotate.

With the info Ivan provided, Camilo's team would surge their advancements when the guards were near the end of their shift, but before the change because they were less attentive at the end of their shift. The team would find places to hide when the shift change happened. The new guards were attentive to every movement and sound at the beginning of their shift until their minds would eventually lose focus so the team timed their movements with the changing of the guards.

Guayo was the first to reach his assigned position on the north flank. He tucked into the crotch of the roots of a massive Matapalo ficus tree. He used some of the large leaves from the jungle floor to cover him as he crouched motionless. A few moments later he could hear the snapping of twigs from the footsteps of an approaching guard.

Guayo focused on his breathing to help him stay still and to center his mind. He peered through a small gap in the leaves to see the black military boots of the guard. The guard's feet stopped one meter to the left of him, right on the other side of the massive root of the tree.

He listened to the sound of a zipper unzipping. Next, he heard the sound of fluid splashing against the root and the ground. The guard had chosen the nature-made stall of the ficus tree roots next to him to relieve himself. When the guard finished, Guayo listened to the zipper again followed by the sound of footsteps fading into the distance.

He was lucky. Had he been discovered, it would mean certain disaster for the op. So far things were going as planned, but it is imperative to keep the streak going.

CHAPTER II
PLACES EVERYONE

With six hours left until the swap, Chepe settled into his perch in the rock outcropping on the south. He had the easiest position to access. It was very easy to stay hidden behind the rocks. He had plenty of room to stretch out and not jeopardize being seen. He definitely won the best position for the op.

Camilo was last to reach his station since his assignment was the most difficult. He had to thread the needle between two guards to the closest place of cover to the house. He had to use the landscaping to skirt the beach between the house and the water. The most eye-catching view from Casa Bamboo was definitely the beach and the ocean. Odds are at least one person from the house would be looking in that direction nearly all the time.

Camilo had to move at a snail's pace to avoid detection. He used natural foliage to create a ghillie suit. The sun was still fairly high, but the shadows were getting longer, providing more shaded spots to advance through.

It took an hour and a half longer for him to get into position, but he was able to navigate the challenge with surprising success. He still had four and a half hours until the swap to remain motionless and pray his body didn't cramp.

Fortunately, the cartel assumed that if there was an attack from the beach it would involve fast boats. They were not expecting swimmers.

At the same time Camilo got into position, Vic and Gordo took flight from the resort. It was an hour and fifteen-minute hop to the airfield nearest the rendezvous point.

"I know she's your mother," said Vic through the helicopter headset, "but look at her, she's a knockout. You can't blame the guy for taking the opportunity."

Gordo gave Vic a look that he did not like where this was going.

"And last I checked, it takes two to tango," she added.

"It is my mother, so it will never be acceptable," defended Gordo. "Even if she was the one who instigated it."

So that was it, that was the reason Gordo was pissed off at The Skipper. He had slept with Gordo's mom. If she did make advances at him, it was unreasonable to expect The Skipper to resist. Gordo's mom can be very persuasive, and The Skipper's resolve is pretty thin when it comes to sexy women.

Victoria didn't know what Gordo expected. The Skipper is a known player, and Gordo's mom is a very attractive older woman. Perhaps the charms of an older woman were just the variety The Skipper was looking for. After all, the average age of his recent lovers was somewhere closer to twenty-five than fifty.

Gordo and Victoria turned their focus to the view of the landscape below which resembled one of those "National Geographic" programs about the rainforests and volcanoes of Costa Rica. For the rest of the flight, they soaked in the beauty beneath them and prepared for the next phase of the plan. The challenges and risks were only going to increase from here. As their eyes surveyed the landscape, their brains couldn't help but be consumed with running through scenarios of events to come.

There was a visible transition as the old forest gave way to the new growth of the secondary forest. This was the land that was reclaimed by the country's efforts to save the natural recourses of the rainforest. Since becoming protected, several acres have sprung back to life with native plants and trees. Before long, the forest gave way to large areas of cleared pastureland. At one time, this whole area was a wild forest.

Gregario's eyes searched the ground wildly as they rolled loosely in their sockets. He drifted in and out of consciousness as the sedation slowly wore off. Vic needed him conscious but wasted for the swap. He didn't put up much fight in this condition, so he was easier to handle. If she let him sober up, it would be difficult to get him to cooperate and the exchange was going to be tricky enough without him adding to it.

As they crossed the small country from north to south, they flew over jungles, volcanoes, pastures, cities, towns, and even beaches. They saw a wide range of sights on the short flight to the Osa Peninsula. They landed at the airfield and loaded into the silver Toyota Prado that was waiting for them.

As Gordo pulled out onto the road following the GPS to the exchange location, Vic checked in with Ivan.

"We're on the road, en route," informed Vic. "We should be there in about an hour. Any updates?"

"Camilo's team is in position," Ivan reported. "So far, none of the cartel men are aware of their presence. We have counted twelve hostiles on-site, but I don't think Leo and Robby are on location so there will probably be at least a few more. The Skipper and Imri are making circles and will get in position when you are less than twenty minutes out."

"Good work," acknowledged Victoria. "I will let you know when we are getting close, and we can switch to comms."

The SUV swung back and forth across the dirt road as Gordo maneuvered to miss as many potholes as possible. Dirt roads in tropical areas become very rutted and rough from frequent rain.

This area of Costa Rica was less inhabited and therefore did not receive the attention to the roads that areas with higher populations did. If you didn't know any better, you might think that the majority of drivers in this region were drunk as they drifted from one side of the road to the other to avoid hazards.

Similar to the helicopter ride, Gregario's eyes searched the landscape as his mind floated along its chemically induced ride. No more doses, at this point Vic just hoped he wouldn't become too lucid and become problematic. For the moment he was relaxed and what he did say was mostly nonsense.

Back at the rendezvous, Camilo's team tried to slowly stretch and change positions as they waited as motionless as possible. Holding the same position for hours causes cramps and pain. They need their muscles to be exceptionally responsive when the time comes. Stretching helps restore blood flow and keep their limbs from falling asleep, but they must be careful to not be seen.

The road narrowed the further Gordo drove. Eventually, there were no more power lines. Leo obviously wanted a secluded location for the exchange. There should be little to no law enforcement in the area. Thankfully, the team's comms did not rely on local infrastructure, so they were able to communicate even off the grid.

"We're about fifteen minutes from the coordinates," Gordo announced.

"I'll let Ivan know to get everyone online," replied Vic.

Ivan sent messages to the team to turn on their comms.

Camilo's team needed to keep quiet to avoid being discovered. They reported they were on by squelching the mic. Once for Camilo, twice for Guayo, and three for Chepe.

"Okay, everyone's on," reported Imri.

"I hope you boys are ready," said Vic.

"Leo is at the location," informed Ivan. "He arrived with Robby and four other guards ten minutes ago."

"What condition is Robby in?" asked Vic. "Can he make it to the chopper?"

"He was escorted by the guards," Robby said. "His hands were bound, but his legs seemed strong. I think he can make the hike through the jungle."

"How's Gregario?" asked Ivan.

"He's conscious but still very disoriented," answered Vic. "We loaded him in the Prado, but

I'm hoping he can walk, and we don't have to drag him to the swap."

"There should be a bottle of caffeine pills in the med bag," Imri chimed in over the coms. "Give him three and it should help bring him out of the sedation. Since you only have a short time before you arrive, the effects may be slight, but it should help."

"Doing it now," replied Vic as she dug through the bag for the pills. "Are you and The Skipper in position?"

"I've got eyes on the boys now," he answered. "The Skipper and a crewman are messing with the poles in the back to keep up appearances. He said he may have a few surprises up his sleeve, whatever that means."

"Knowing him I'm not sure whether to be encouraged or scared," said Vic.

Gordo followed the winding road through the thick forest as they approached the location. Capuchin monkeys jumped from tree to tree as they crossed the road above the SUV. The rugged terrain made a path through the wilderness full of life. They turned down a narrow driveway with ruts and rocks shaking the Prado until the trees gave way to an opening and they were able to see the structures for the first time.

"We're pulling in now," announced Vic.

"The roaming guards have doubled," updated Ivan. "There are two to the north, two to the south, and four that are staying close to the opening at the front of the property. We tracked four guards who walked back down the road a bit. You will pass them on your way in. I assume they will be trying to prevent your escape."

"We did not see them on the way in," said Vic "They must have been hiding off the road in the bushes."

Gordo pulled into the small parking area and searched for a way to park the car while leaving an escape route. It wasn't possible, there was not enough room to turn around quickly. If they needed to flee in the car, they would have to do it in reverse. It didn't really matter; they weren't planning on leaving in the Prado anyway. But it would have been nice to leave the option open just in case their plans changed.

Vic and Gordo took a few deep breaths as they surveyed the area from the relative safety of the vehicle. They took note of the location of the guards they could see and the weapons they held.

There seemed to be a mixture of two groups. Each pair of guards had one man dressed in tactical gear and the others wore suits. Apparently, each Gulf Cartel member had a CAC counterpart.

"Take out the men in tactical gear first," instructed Vic. "Assuming they are part of the CAC, they should be better trained."

"Copy," acknowledged Imri. Camilo's team stayed silent.

The team watched as men began to emerge from the cabina. She didn't recognize the first two men, but the third was Robby who was being escorted by Leo and then two more guards. These men were all dressed in tactical gear. Vic and Gordo were going to have a tough time with this group.

Leo guided Robby to the middle of the clearing where they stopped and waited for Vic and company to exit the car.

Vic looked to her right and saw a break in the trees. There was a small path that lead back into the jungle in the direction of the river.

"See that opening to my right?" asked Vic. "That's our exit route. As soon as we have Robby, we need to disappear down that path."

"Roger that," answered Gordo as he nonchalantly scanned the edge of the clearing for the path.

"Ready?" asked Vic.

"Let's do this," answered Vic.

"Coming out now," Vic announced over the comms.

CHAPTER 12
THE EXCHANGE

As the Prado door swung open, the loud chattering of the scarlet macaws mixed with the lapping sound of the waves crashing on the beach. With her BCM carbine in hand, Vic opened the back door and grabbed Gregario by the arm.

"Are we there?" he asked deliriously.

"Yes, we are," answered Vic. "Your friends are right over there."

His eyes strained as he looked out into the bright clearing where the men were standing about 30 meters away. Vic let out a slight sigh of relief as he stepped out of the Prado. The caffeine had worked enough that he was able to walk now.

She directed him to the front of the car where

Gordo was standing with his DDM4 at the ready. Gordo's eyes scanned the group, watching for movement. Gregario swayed slightly as he tried to find equilibrium. Vic stood at Gregario's side with her pistol pointed at his ribs.

"Bring him to me," instructed Leo.

"I don't think so," answered Vic. "They walk at the same time."

"Fine," replied Leo with a slight grin. He felt very comfortable that they had nowhere to go. Still, he didn't trust Victoria.

Standing in the tropical air, Vic began to sweat beneath her tactical vest with bulletproof plates. The gear was slightly heavy and quite warm, but she would endure some discomfort to protect herself and carry her arsenal.

"Start walking," Leo commanded.

Robby looked at Leo, turned back to Victoria, and took a step. He was gagged and his hands were zip-tied but his legs were free. Vic took note and her mind checked her blade strapped to her vest. She would need to cut him free quickly so that he could use his hands as they fled. Vic kept hold of Gregario until Robby had taken a few steps her way.

"Send him now," Leo demanded.

Vic nudged Gregario, "Go to your people," she said calmly. He was cooperating and she didn't want to cause him any reason to get upset. His eyes drifted slowly from Vic to the group of men in the clearing and the one walking his way. He began stumbling in their direction.

"You go as fast as he goes," Leo said to Robby who slowed his stride to match the pace of Gregario.

Vic followed Gregario with her Pistol as the men reached the halfway mark. Gregario looked at Robby quizzically as the two passed. Robby's legs were shaky and his eyes searched Vic's for instruction while pleading for help.

Camilo breathed deeply as he alternated his focus between Robby and the guard in his sights. The earthy smell of damp ground filled his nostrils. His finger rested gently on the trigger of his M4. With slightly tensed muscles, he prepared to strike.

"Two rafts with gunmen just appeared running the coast north toward your location!" Ivan shouted through the comms.

"I don't like the looks of this," said The Skipper as he peered through his Nikon 8252 Aculon long-range binoculars.

Imri agreed, "We are way outgunned. I don't see how we can get Vic's team out; they are going to get slaughtered."

"Bring me the sea-wiz controls," he yelled at the crewman who quickly snapped into action.

One of the many upgrades that The Skipper had added to his superyacht was a Phalanx CIWS 20 mm M61 Vulcan Gatling gun autocannon. His Navy buddies installed the CIWS gun-based close-in weapon system, referred to as the sea-wiz, to defend the yacht against incoming threats such as aircraft, missiles, and small boats.

Although the sea-wiz generally uses auto-targeting software to lock on and eliminate targets, The Skipper needed to make sure there was no friendly fire that would take out the team members. During the sea-wiz installation, his buddies made a few modifications including an optic headset that allows an operator to visually identify and target threats.

Moments later the young crewman reappeared with the headset and controls in hand. So as not to draw attention, the sea-wiz was mounted to a platform that retracted below the roof of the yacht. It rose out the top of the craft as The Skipper donned the headset and assumed control of the weapon.

"We have to wait for Vic's signal!" Imri cautioned. "She doesn't have Rob..."

The Skipper was quick to cut him off, "If the boats get in range, they will all be dead. We don't have time to wait. Once I begin firing our cover is blown. Eliminate anyone aiming our way."

"Everyone Get Down," The Skipper instructed over the comms.

Imri returned his focus to his scope and scanned for targets. The technology of the sea-wiz headset highlighted potential targets. The Skipper marked a couple of the men in tactical gear surrounding Leo and then he turned the focus to the approaching boats. As he pulled the trigger, the R2D2-looking weapon jerked the cluster of barrels toward the beach. The barrel spun up and began spewing lead. The air filled with a sound similar to a buzzsaw and sparks shot from the revolving barrels. It was loud!

Hearing The Skipper's abrupt instructions, Vic lunged forward toward Robby. He had no way of receiving the warning, so it was up to Vic to get him to the ground. It was obvious that The Skipper was not going to wait for Robby to get to cover before engaging. As she leaped toward him, she yelled, "¡Bajar!"

The first to fall were the two men on Leo's right followed by another two guards to the south near Chepe. The weapon swung violently to catch up to the next target. The Skipper had the sights of the headset trained on the raft nearest the team. Following the targeting program as quickly as The Skipper could push the fire button, the onslaught of rounds fell on the craft. It quickly deflated and sank leaving the remaining three gunmen who didn't get hit to swim for shore.

Robby was about five paces from Vic when the barrage of bullets erupted. Another CAC member to Leo's right began to raise his rifle to shoot. Before the man could get the rifle up to aim Camilo's finger squeezed the trigger, and he dropped him. Vic tackled Robby to the ground with her back to the gunman.

At the sound of gunfire, Leo instinctually grabbed Gregario and raced for the safety of the cabin. The remaining guards near Leo flanked the two men and provided cover fire as they escorted the bosses to the structure.

A lightning bolt of pain shocked Vic's left shoulder blade as it took a round from a guard near Guayo. Her vest had kept the slug from piercing her skin, but the impact was excruciating. Fighting the urge to flex her back, Vic bore down, flexed her abdomen, and cradled Robby, shielding him from the cartel men. A second later the location of Vic's pain shifted as another bullet slammed into the middle of her spine.

Identifying his next target, Guayo trained his weapon on the one shooting at Vic. Guayo squeezed the trigger and the gangster fell before he could get off another round. Just then, a bullet whizzed past his ear and Guayo ducked back in to cover to determine the location of the shooter. Weapon at the ready he popped back up and with color in his sights squeezed the trigger rapidly dropping his third target.

In seconds, the gunmen on the second raft changed course and headed toward the "World is Not Enough." Through the mist spraying from the bow of the raft as it pushed over the waves, Imri sighted the driver. It was very difficult with the sea motion of both vessels. He timed the bobbing action of the boats and delivered a clean headshot from 75 meters.

The raft drifted off course for a moment until one of the gunmen was able to take the controls.

The other men fired at the yacht. The crack of the bullets striking the fiberglass could be heard between the intermittent BRAAP sounds of the sea-wiz.

"Get this boat underway!" shouted The Skipper at the helmsman who engaged the engine controls.

The adrenaline and endorphins pumping through Vic's veins provided minimal relief from the searing pain in her back. As she huddled on the ground, she took control of her mind. Much like the art of meditation, she had learned how to change her focus and place her attention on her surroundings rather than what was happening to her body.

Sensing an opening, Vic rose and grabbed Robby pulling him to his feet. "Move," she yelled, pushing Robby toward the Prado as she fired over her shoulder in the direction of the nearest cartel men. When the shooting started, Gordo sought the cover of the SUV. He peered around the corner, firing at targets and tracking Gregario as he made his way into the cabin. He provided cover fire for Vic and Robby who dove for the protection of the Prado.

Gordo shouted at Vic, "You good?"

"Good enough," replied Vic.

Robby coughed and gasped for air. After removing his gag, Vic pulled her Adamas knife and sliced the zip ties that bound Robby's hands. "We're getting out of here," Vic instructed as she looked deep into Robby's eyes which were filled with horror. "I'm going to lead the way and Gordo here is going to cover our backs."

Robby nodded acknowledgment which contradicted the lost look on his face. He had never heard a gun fired in real life, let alone the vast arsenal that was being unloaded on the beach. The only thing drowning out his racing pulse pounding in his ears was the various clack and bang sounds of the semi-automatic weapons and that strange buzz coming from the ship in the bay. He was doing his best not to freeze in fear.

The floral smells of the jungle were replaced with gunpowder, and the hazy ocean mist was changed to a filter of smoke and muzzle flashes. This tropical paradise had become the scene of nightmares. The blood of the fallen pulled the focus from the beauty of the exotic plants and ocean vistas.

With Vic and Robby to his back, Gordo darted out from cover to eliminate a gunman targeting

Chepe who was pinned down between a pair of guards and the gunman approaching from the beach. He had eradicated two CACs and one Gulf and was holding his own against surmounting bad odds.

The "World is Not Enough" led the raft away from the rest of the team on the beach. With the yacht racing away from the raft, the gunmen were less effective in hitting their target. The Skipper directed his weapon at the pursuing raft. With the raft in his sights, The Skipper pushed the red button, and the sea-wiz began its purr.

The raft and its passengers were shredded by the Gatling gun. It would have been simple for The Skipper to let the sea-wiz autotarget the raft, but there was satisfaction in using the manual targeting. The Skipper released the red button and watched the pieces of destruction sink into the ocean.

"Get us back to the beach!" shouted The Skipper at the helmsman. The yacht came about and made course just off the coast from the team. Imri waited eagerly as the beach grew closer in his scope. He was still out of range, but they were closing fast. Just not as fast as the raft team was closing on Chepe.

"If you don't get me in range, Chepe's dead!" yelled Imri.

"10 seconds kid!" The Skipper hollered back.

"He'll be dead in 5!" bellowed Imri.

Guayo had eliminated the majority of targets in his sector. The others were taken out by Camilo and Gordo. With his area clear, he made his way toward Camilo's location to try to help out.

Miniature dirt explosions erupted around Camilo as the men sprayed the area with lead. He was pinned down by the gunmen in the cabins. At one point he had Gregario in his sights but missed high right. In addition to the bullets coming from the buildings, his exit was blocked by a couple of the guards who were shooting at Chepe.

Vic grabbed Robby by the arm, "Let's move, stay with me!" she shouted at him. She pushed off the side of the SUV and made a run for the tree line. Robby followed Vic while Gordo kept constant fire as he moved from one target to the next.

CHAPTER 13
FIREFIGHT AT SUNSET

Trunks and limbs cracked as bullets tore through the foliage all around Vic's team. She broke through the thick bushes as they pushed their way deeper into the jungle. They needed to get more cover between them and the gunman and reach the stream about fifty meters from the road.

Guayo and Camilo kept their fire focused on the doors to the structures. This kept the cartel men from chasing Vic's team into the jungle for the moment. They could hear Leo shouting at the men inside as he expressed his anger that the group was getting away.

"The men sent to guard the road are headed

back to your location," Ivan updated. "They are avoiding the buildings and seem focused on the pursuit of Vic's team."

The incoming rounds subsided a bit as Vic's team gained some distance into the thick forest. It was enough for them to regroup for a second. Ducking behind a large Cyprus tree, Vic put her hands on either side of Robby's face and locked eyes with him.

"I know you are scared; I know you are not trained for this, but I need you to listen." Vic had a gift for being able to take control and provide focus amid chaos. "We have a helicopter to escape, we just have to get there before these men catch us. If you stop, you will be killed. If you follow my orders, I promise I will get you to that chopper alive. I need you to pull your shit together and do as I say. Do you understand?"

Robby's expression changed as he took in Victoria's words. Her eyes provided solace and strength. For her, he could become whomever she needed. He would find courage where he had none. He believed in her enough that it made him feel empowered. He would show her he could control his fear. He would be brave in the face of death.

"I understand," Robby replied with a nod.

Not wasting another second, Vic gave the order, "Let's move!" The group continued their push for the stream that would lead them to their getaway. The trio followed a narrow path around a bend in a small canyon. The path was overgrown, and the canopy blocked much of the sun. The surrounding walls of the canyon shot rays of sunlight through the gaps in the branches while the center of the bend was fully lit with the colors of the sunset. A dozen Blue Morpho butterflies danced in the sunlight as they fluttered their ascent toward a waterfall deeper in the canyon. They were seemingly oblivious to the gunfight.

The trail veered off as it approached the waterfall. Through the vista of the canyon, Gordo, who was covering the rear, spotted their pursuers. The men from the road had located the trail and were pushing hard to catch up to the escapees. Fortunately for Vic's team, they all appeared to be Gulf Cartel. They wore jeans and button-down shirts rather than tactical gear. These men did not have the same combat training but were basic thugs and hired guns.

"We've got to get him out of there!" yelled Imri to The Skipper.

"If we let those men out of that cabina they will go after Vic!" The Skipper yelled back. "The mission is to get Robby to the chopper."

"Camilo, can you hold your position?" Imri asked.

"I'm pinned down at the moment," Camilo yelled over the gunfire. "I'm not going anywhere."

Finally in range, Imri lined up a shot for the boat gunman closest to Chepe. Chepe was in the crossfire from the boatmen on the southeast and the Gulf men on the northwest that was blocking Camilo's exit. Occasionally one of the gunmen who retreated to the structures would take a shot at him as well. Imri squeezed the trigger just as a wave sideswiped the superyacht. He missed but it was enough to cause the guard to duck for cover.

Chepe randomly popped up from behind the various rocks. He was doing an incredible job of taking shots without getting hit. But there was no mistaking he was in trouble and his odds were worsening by the second. Turning toward the boat crew that was approaching from behind, he sprung up and was able to get a clean shot on one of them. Blood sprayed from the neck of his target as he fell backward grabbing for the wound on the way down. Chepe dropped back into cover just as bullets ricocheted off the rocks at what was head height a moment before.

"Aim for the Gulfs between Camilo and Chepe!" directed The Skipper. "That will allow Camilo an escape route and help Chepe."

Imri took the suggestion and lined up for a shot on the cartel men. This time the bullet landed exactly where he aimed, square in the back of the gunman's head. A moment later Guayo landed a shot in the leg of the other Gulf member. Following the man to the ground, Guayo's muzzle flared as he finished him off.

"From the satellite feed, the thermal images look like Gregario is being dragged out the back window by a couple of men." Reported Ivan. "They are making a break for the SUVs. I count four men. It looks like there are still two men in the structure nearest the beach."

The Black Toyota drove through a small hedge as it swung onto the small dirt drive that led away from the property. That was at least three fewer guns showering Camilo and company with lead.

The low-hanging sun provided a yellow-orange glare that bounced across the tops of the waves as it blazed onto the shore. The bright light made it an optimal time for Camilo's team to withdraw and attempt their escape. The blinding glare made it difficult for the cartel men to identify targets and take aim.

Laying belly down on the roof of the yacht next to Imri, The Skipper grabbed a rifle and took aim on the beach. "Camilo, it's time to get your team out of there!" commanded The Skipper. "We'll provide cover fire, but you are going to have to get off the beach quickly."

The frogmen need to retreat to the water for extraction by The Skipper's crew. With the attack boats incapacitated, their swim to the pickup point shouldn't be a problem. "Ready the rescue raft for launch," The Skipper commanded the boatswain. "Be prepared for a quick grab and tell the helmsman to be ready to get us the hell out of here."

"Chepe, the path toward Camilo is clear to the north," informed Imri, "I will cover the men to the south. try to get to Camilo's location and the three of you can get to the beach from there."

With the sun to their backs, Imri focused his fire on the CAC men near Chepe while The Skipper aimed at the doors and windows of the cabinas.

The Skipper's rifle was not very accurate at this range, but it worked to keep the men in the structures at bay while the team worked on their egress.

Seeing the rounds from the bay pelting the rocks and plants around the hostiles, Chepe sprung from cover and made a run toward Camilo. Guayo and Camilo alternated their suppression fire between the cabina and the men in the brush. Reaching the edge of the clearing, Chepe slid out of sight behind a bright green alocasia plant.

Camilo looked at the other two warriors and cracked a grin. "Let's get out of here, hermanos!" He was proud of his brothers in arms. His friends had helped get Robby back and they had kicked some ass in the process. The team of three established formation and began their retreat toward the water.

Vic spun and began firing back at their pursuers. The men had gained on them, and they were back in firing range. They were almost a hundred meters from the helicopter.

"You're almost there," Ivan encouraged over coms. "The chopper is spun up and ready to take off as soon as you load."

"We're comin' in hot," replied Vic.

"I see that," replied Ivan. "The flight crew has been instructed to cover your egress. Good luck."

The helicopter was in a clearing just over the ridge. To load, they would need to cross an open area fully exposed. Without trees and shrubs to disguise their movements and deflect bullets, they would need to move fast to avoid being shot by the gunmen while in the open.

"Give me a gun!" Robby asserted.

His expression had changed since Vic checked in on him last. The chase through the thick vegetation had consumed her focus. The terror and confusion had slipped away. Somehow Robby was dealing with his situation and ready to engage in its outcome. There was the confidence she had not seen since the dancefloor where he projected his machismo.

Firing around him at the figure that peered around a large fig tree, Vic handed the VP9 in her right hand to him. The weapon was a full-size 9 mil with a solid controlled feel. It was easier to shoot than the compact P365XL in her other hand.

"Only fire after you've aimed," she said. "Don't waste bullets on bad shots."

The simple instruction without reservation

prodded Robby's confidence. And it was great advice. The more she believed in him, the more he believed in himself. It was clear he considered her Maestra.

The first round pierced his shoulder before Gordo's second bullet tore a chunk from the cartel member's skull. The gunman had focused on Vic and Robby leaving an opening for Gordo to take him out. With Robby now armed, it was three on three. But a shootout was not the mission, getting Robby and everyone else out safely was the objective.

The three continued to push for the helo, only returning fire to slow their hunters. Following Vic and Gordo's lead, Robby would peek out from behind trees to take shots at the men following them. As instructed, he made a conscious effort not to pull the trigger until he had a target in his sights. He did not hit any of the men, but the simple act of aiming and firing a weapon at a human was something.

The experience of his capture had changed him. The look of terror wasn't at the forefront of his expression anymore. He showed bravery and courage. No longer was he one who would sit idly by and let others push him around. It was clear he was not the same man that had been taken a few days ago.

Approaching the edge of the clearing, Gordo found a position to hold the men off a moment. He slammed a new magazine into his DDM4 and he began pinning their pursuers behind the cover of trees and rocks. This stopped their advance and provided a few seconds for Vic and Robby to load.

"Go, go, go," yelled Vic, pushing Robby into the clearing toward the chopper.

The crewman had stepped from the helicopter and was firing his rifle at the men in the trees. He stopped firing long enough to extend a hand to Robby to assist him in climbing into the helicopter. Not giving the crewman time to assist, Vic jumped in right behind Robby.

"Get us in the air!" commanded Vic.

"What about him?" asked the pilot.

"He'll catch up," yelled Vic. "Get us out of here!"

Without a response, the pilot turned his focus to the windshield and began to pull back on the stick. The crewman jumped in, and they began to levitate. Vic grabbed a fast-rope and clipped the end to the tiedown point outside the door. The helicopter began to climb as she kicked the coil of rope out the opening. The rope unraveled with only a small section laying on the ground.

"Gordo, time to go," Vic said over coms.

She grabbed the rifle from the crewman and began cover fire for Gordo's escape. Hearing the order, Gordo immediately spun around and ran for the leaving helicopter. He grabbed the rope moments before the end left the ground. Climbing up a bit he wrapped his legs around the rope and locked himself in position. This was nothing new for Gordo. One of his favorite tactical approaches was spie rigging - method involving military men clipping themselves to a rope descended from an attack helicopter and flown into battle.

As they ascended the men risked exposing themselves to Vic's rifle fire to take some shots at the dangling target. A few rounds struck the hull of the helicopter but did not hit anything affecting flight. The slide flew back and forth, ejecting hot shells as Vic continued to return fire. The distance grew and it would only be a few moments until they were out of range.

Gordo wouldn't have to hold on long. As soon as they were a safe distance from the gunman, the pilot would find a place to set down and let him climb inside. In the meantime, Gordo felt a bit like a superhero. The mission was a success, they had recovered Robby and he was flying away without injury. He hoped the team on the beach was having similar success.

CHAPTER 14
DARK WATER

The sun sat just above the water as the day drew to a close. The remaining gunman continued to engage with Camilo's team. The opposing sides exchanged shots as darkness descended on the beach.

"Apparently, someone reported your fireworks, Skipper," Ivan said. "The Coast Guard has been dispatched to your location. They are about ten minutes away."

"Understood," replied The Skipper. "Send the raft to the beach," he commanded the boatswain.

"Camilo, time's up. Get your team to the water," directed The Skipper.

As he finished, the raft circled the stern of the yacht and raced toward the shore. The boatswain was accompanied by another crewman with a rifle. The raft rose and fell with the rolling tide. The low light helped disguise its approach.

The remaining cartel men gave chase to the team's retreat. The beach nearest Camilo's team had a long shallow reef before dropping into deeper water. The gunman would cut them down trying to cross the shallows before they got a chance to begin their swim.

They needed to make their way back to where Guayo had made his landing. To get there, they needed to cross a small opening and race through the jungle to a rock outcropping. From the rocks they could drop into the water where the raft would be waiting a few meters away.

Camilo's team huddled behind a rotted wooden kayak stand littered with kayaks, paddles, and life vests. "I'm down to my last magazine," reported Camilo.

"Me too," replied Chepe.

"I have two," said Guayo and he handed one of them to Camilo.

Camilo tucked the magazine into his belt. "Our only way out is the way you came in," Camilo looked at Guayo as he spoke. "Lead us out."

Guayo nodded, tapped Chepe on the shoulder,

and started down the path along the coast. Chepe followed and fell in behind him with his weapon at the ready. Camilo trailed Chepe, covering their retreat while conserving ammo as much as possible.

With the team together, the cartel men concentrated on their single location and were closing in. Imri was not able to take out the men in the cabina as they made a break for the cover of the jungle. The rolling of the yacht proved more difficult to maintain his aim than he had anticipated. The assault from Imri and The Skipper did keep the men from openly charging after the team though. The gunmen dashed and ducked from one obstacle to another to avoid the sniper fire.

Once the men crossed the clearing, Imri lost sight of them in the jungle. "I've lost visual of all hostiles," he reported over coms.

"We're in the clear," Victoria announced. She pulled her comms from her ear and passed it to Robby.

"Primo?" Robby asked. "Estoy bien."

"Gracias a Dios," replied Camilo.

Vic knew Camilo needed to hear from Robby. It was important he knew his cousin made it out alive. It was difficult for him not to be on the team to get Robby to safety, but he knew that Vic needed to handle the exchange with Gregario. His place was to provide distraction and cover fire to help his cousin slip away.

Vic reached out and asked for the comms back. "Get home safe, mi hermano," she said.

This was not the time for chatter. Camilo and his team needed to focus their attention on avoiding the incoming fire and getting to the water. The gunmen were advancing quickly. They needed to keep moving or they would be pinned down with no escape.

Shots whizzed over their heads as the team used a fallen tree to shield them. The cartel men continued to advance and had reduced their distance to nearly thirty meters.

"Go, go, go..." yelled Camilo, popping around the exposed roots of the fallen tree. Through the unearthed maze of roots, he was able to get a clear shot at one of their pursuers as the other two sprang from cover and dashed for their next shield. Camilo's bullet hit the gunman in the left arm, knocking him to the ground. Capitalizing on the moment, Camilo jumped up and raced to join his teammates behind a Pochote tree.

"The men that were chasing Vic have doubled

back and are coming at you from the north," reported Ivan. "They are about sixty meters away and closing fast. If they get to the beach, they will have a line of sight on your rendezvous point with the raft."

"We'll cover best we can," The Skipper interjected. "If they show themselves on the beach, we should be able to hold them off for a bit." Imri swung the barrel of the sniper rifle to scan the beach north of the rock outcropping.

Guayo pulled some paracord from his vest and made a quick spring trap with the rubber tree across from them. Even if the trap did not stop the cartel men, it should slow them for a moment. The thick leaves cast shadows across the path allowing the trip cord to disappear into the silhouettes. With the end of the cord secured across the path, the team moved out and made their surge for the rocks.

Guayo led the charge from the trees across the small patch of sand and out onto the rocks. Chepe followed a few paces back with Camilo right on his heels. Guayo searched the north beach for the other group of cartel men while Camilo kept his rifle trained on the path behind them.

As Guayo's left boot made contact with the

sand, he spied a gunman emerging from the trees to the north. Without breaking stride, he pointed his rifle in the direction of the men and began taking shots. Imri and The Skipper joined in from offshore. The barrage of bullets only slowed the men slightly.

It was clear these men were told they would be killed if they allowed anyone to escape. In the cartel, there are few options. You are given orders and either you obey, or you die. Aside from their loyalty to their organization, the men feared punishment for not doing their jobs more than the men they combatted.

Chepe joined the fusillade on the team to the north. Behind them, a rustle of leaves could be heard as the men following them tripped the trap. The long flexible branch of the rubber tree sprung from tension. The sweeping arc caught the leader in the side and threw him against the Pochote tree. The force of his head slamming against the tree forced the strong spikes along the trunk to puncture his ear and the side of his face. The man fell to the ground grabbing his face as blood ran into his right eye obscuring his vision. The others stepped over him as they continued their pursuit, guns blazing.

The sprung trap let Camilo know their attackers were close and he began to fire down the path behind them. The gunman in the raft helped hold the men to the north at bay as Guayo made a leap for the water. The boatswain extended an ore to pull Guayo to the raft. As he hefted Guayo into the raft Chepe made his rush for the water.

Camilo continued to hold off the men to the rear as The Skipper, Imri, and the raft crewman focused their fire to the north. Using his strong legs to propel him, Chepe's boots sunk into the sand as he leaned forward and pushed for the rocks. In desperation, the men on the beach exposed themselves to take shots at the fleeing warriors.

Jumping for the rocks, Chepe's vest absorbed the impact of two rounds to the back. The force of the projectiles spun him in the air. A third round found a soft spot between the front and back plates. The spinning had exposed Chepe's side to the direction of fire providing a small opening to the vulnerability of his ribcage.

Chepe's body fell limp and rolled off the rocks, his momentum carrying him into the water. Camilo saw the window closing on his exit and made a break for the water. The crewman maintained his fire on the hostiles while Guayo and the boatswain attempted to fish Chepe from the dark water.

Chepe's mouth gurgled, full of blood and water. The light of the moon illuminated his eyes which were wide with pain and fear. The searing pain in his chest told him that he was not going to survive this one.

"Hang in there, buddy," encouraged the boatswain. Guayo pulled a gauze pad from his med kit and stuffed it into the side of Chepe's vest against the wound. He did not offer words; he knew there was nothing he could offer Chepe at this point.

A barrage of bullets surrounded Camilo as the only remaining target. Three quick steps and he launched himself from the rocks. Diving into the water, he took a round to the chest before splashing into the water. He struggled his way to the surface, fighting for oxygen as the impact of the bullet in the vest had pushed the air from his lungs and caused his chest muscles to constrict.

"Keep firing," yelled The Skipper, "We have to keep them from advancing onto the beach!"

"Louis, grab a gun!" The Skipper ordered. "Aim for those flashing lights on the beach!"

Without questioning the order, the chef grabbed a rifle from a hidden compartment and began firing at the muzzle flashes in the darkness along the tree line. Imri continued to try to time the rolling waves. He was able to graze one of the cartel men causing him to fall to the ground momentarily. Using the thermal scope, he reported the locations of targets to The Skipper and Louis.

With Guayo's help, Camilo rolled over the side of the raft. With everyone onboard, the boatswain returned to the helm and headed the raft toward the yacht. Bullets splashed the water on either side of the raft. The boatswain did his best to serpentine his course to make it more difficult for the gunman.

"Chepe?" Camilo asked, struggling to regain his breath.

"No es bueno hermano," replied Guayo.

With one hand holding pressure on Chepe's wound, Guayo used his other to fire his rifle at the shore. The large moon shined bright across the water exposing the raft in the darkness. The moon's mass pulled at the water generating large waves that would crest and fall. The raft lifted from the tops and slammed into the troughs.

Working his way to his knees, Camilo rejoined the firefight against the shore.

Click... "I'm out!" shouted Guayo. He turned his focus on Chepe. He applied another gauze and increased the pressure on the wound. It was a futile effort, and he knew it. But he had to do something.

Click... Camilo's rifle emptied as well. "Give me your rifle!" he demanded of the crewman.

It was quite apparent that this was not a man to argue with. The crewman knew that the man was a soldier as opposed to a simple boat crew. Sure, The Skipper had given him some arms training, but he was no spec ops operator. He handed over the weapon and ducked for cover as he held on to keep from being thrown from the raft.

As the raft grew closer, The Skipper noticed lights in the water, approaching from the north.

"Get us underway," The Skipper instructed the helmsmen. "We will need to snatch them up as we go."

The helmsmen set a course to intercept the raft while sustaining the direction of escape from the fast-approaching craft. It took an agonizing 90 seconds to reach the raft. That doesn't sound like much time unless you are in the middle of a firefight with dwindling ammo. The superyacht took hits from the beach as it shielded the raft.

The helmsman adjusted his course away from the Coast Guard ship towards the open water. The ship's horn could be heard piercing the darkness as a warning. They had turned on their spotlight and it was clear they intended to detain The Skipper and crew.

CHAPTER 15
LOOSE ENDS AND LEFTOVERS

The vibrations of the helicopter helped Vic to relax a bit as they gained distance from the action. With Robby safely on board and no one on her team injured, she was pleased with the outcome of the mission so far. She prayed Camillo's team was having similar success.

Taking stock of the situation, she tried to identify any loose ends she may have overlooked. It was disappointing that she had to give up Gregario, but through the interrogation, she felt he knew what he had done to deserve her vengeance. Reflecting on the events that led her to this point, she was struck with the realization that she had placed someone in greater danger than before she had questioned Gregario.

Victoria sent a message to Ivan, "Can you get me a location for Alejandra?"

A few minutes later she received a message from Priya. "Ivan said you are looking for Alejandra. I have been tracking her since she boarded the plane in Caicos after the exchange. The last visual was outside the farmhouse where you and Camilo followed the trucks."

"Thanks, Priya," replied Vic.

"My pleasure," Priya responded. "Let me know how I can help."

"Get me as much intel as possible on that farmhouse," Vic directed. "I need to know how many men are guarding the location. And find me a place nearby where we can set the chopper down without the guards knowing we're near."

"On it," acknowledged Priya. "I will see if Ivan can get me satellite or drone coverage of the area."

Vic put her phone back in her pocket and grabbed the headphones hanging on the bulkhead. She pointed to Robby and Gordo and tapped her ear indicating she wanted them to put on headphones so she could talk to them without yelling over the noise of the helicopter rotors.

"I need you to take Robby home and wait with him until Camilo or I get there," Vic instructed Gordo.

"Why? Where are you going?" he asked with a puzzled look.

"I made a promise to protect someone," explained Vic, "if I don't go get them now, Gregario will soon kill them."

"Don't you need backup?" asked Gordo.

"I've already put too many people in jeopardy. It's more important that you keep Robby safe."

"Don't worry about me," objected Robby, still holding Vic's VP9, "you need someone to watch your back. I'll be fine."

"Thanks, buddy, but I can't take that risk. Your cousin would kill me if I left you unprotected until he returns, and I couldn't live with myself if someone hurt you again."

Robby could see that Vic was not going to change her plans. "You know it's a bad idea to go alone, I wish you weren't so stubborn. You're a badass, but you can't save the world all by yourself."

"Thanks for caring about me guys, but I can handle myself. I promise I'll be careful," Vic said confidently. "Besides, it's easier for one person to go undetected."

With the boys reluctantly conceding, she switched channels to speak to the pilot. Vic conveyed coordinates and instructed the pilot to head for the farmhouse where Gregario's men had taken the kids that had failed inspection. The pilot told her they should get there in thirty-seven minutes. Vic took a moment to consider which weapons she wanted to take. She and Gordo had exhausted their ammo for the ARs. It didn't matter much; she was hoping to be able to get to Alejandra without alerting the cartel men that she was there. Firing her rifle would give away her presence. If she was discovered, she would try to liberate a rifle from one of the guards.

She would need to move quickly and unrestricted. She took off the vest and stripped her gear down to her Adamas survival knife and Sig Saur P365 XL Romeozero. The 9mil was lightweight and the optics would help her aim in the dark without a laser giving away her position. Mostly she was planning on incapacitating the guards with martial arts. If she could sneak up on them and render them unconscious it would keep the others from hearing her attack.

A few minutes later, Priya messaged Vic to let her know that Ivan hacked a satellite and was able to get her thermal images of the area. She advised her to land about a half mile away on the other side of the hill from the farmhouse.

"There is a wind farm that you will need to watch out for, but you should be able to set the helicopter down in a clearing to the east of the structure. You will have to hike over the hill through the wind turbines, but it shouldn't be too difficult since the area was clear-cut for the cattle to graze. I'm sending you the coordinates now."

"Thanks, Priya. Were you able to tell how many guards are there?"

"Unfortunately, I was not. It is too dark to make out any people with the standard optics and thermal showed about 25 heat signatures at the location. I assume the two hot spots at the front and one at the back of the building are guards, but I cannot tell how many on the inside are threats and how many are prisoners."

"One more thing," Priya added, "besides the large cattle, I saw two small hot spots in the fields around the building. I think they are dogs."

"Thanks for the heads up. Good work on the intel, especially with the short notice."

"My pleasure. I'll be standing by in case you need anything else. Good luck."

While Victoria was corresponding with Priya, Robby and Gordo exchanged small talk as they tried to get to know each other a bit better. They found some common ground in their appreciation for cold beer and extreme dislike of the Brazilian fútbol team.

As the chopper raced through the night sky, Vic tried to think of how she could eliminate the threat of the dogs. She could not afford them to alert the guards of her approach. Taking out humans was one thing, but animals were something different.

Growing up in Central America, Vic was raised knowing that dogs were usually more of a security system than pets. Often the animals were mistreated and neglected. Their purpose was to ward off unwanted wildlings like jungle cats, snakes, skunks, and raccoons; as well as, to keep strangers off the property. Unlike much of the world, in Costa Rica, many dogs were not kept in fences or on leashes. They roamed their territory and chased off any unwelcome guests.

Vic relayed the new coordinates to the pilot and warned him about the wind turbines. She told him to swing wide around the farm to avoid the sound of the helicopter reaching the farmhouse. The pilot said he was familiar with the area and would approach from behind the ridge which should help block the sound of the helicopter.

Vic noticed a cooler strapped to the floor next to the pilot. She leaned forward and asked the pilot, "What's in the cooler?"

"I told my wife I wasn't sure what time I would be home, so she packed me dinner," he replied.

"Do you know what she packed?"

"It is leftovers from yesterday. We had arroz con pollo, patacones, and frijoles," he answered. "Why do you ask?"

"I was wondering if you might be willing to give it up. My friend Robby here can get you a nice meal when you land," Vic responded. She knew Robby would not have a problem utilizing his skills in hospitality.

"I imagine you must be hungry after what I saw back there," the pilot said. "You can have it."

"Thanks," said Vic. She proceeded to unstrap the cooler and pull out the contents.

"Robby, when we land can you give the pilot some dinner?" she asked.

"No problem, I am sure my tía Rosa will have something prepared. She is always cooking.

She opened the plastic container with the arroz con pollo and began to pick out the pieces of chicken. Reaching for her vest she pulled open the Velcro flap and removed a small bottle from the top pocket. She poured out a couple of tablets and tucked the bottle into her pant pocket. Gordo and Robby watch with curiosity as she uses her knife to cut the pills in half. The vibration of the helicopter makes the task a bit difficult, but she manages to get the small pieces she needs. Vic takes the bits of tablet and inserts them into the chunks of chicken. She passes the utensils, frijoles, patacones, and rice to Gordo and Robby.

Seeing their quizzical expression she says, "Eat up, I'm sure you boys are hungry."

Of course, they were hungry. They didn't understand why she pulled the best part out of the arroz con pollo, but they weren't about to turn down some food. As they dug into the containers and dipped the patacones into the frijoles. With a mouthful of food, Gordo had to ask, "What are you planning to do with that chicken?"

"Yeah, Vic. That's the best part," added Robby.

"Sorry boys, I am meeting some new friends

who may be a little high-strung," she answered with a grin. She placed the chicken pieces in a zip-lock from the cooler and tucked them into her pocket.

"There wouldn't happen to be a cold cerveza in that cooler you got there," asked Robby.

Vic reached into the cooler and pulled out an Aloe Water. Sorry buddy, this is the best I got.

"Well," Robby said with a shrug, "I guess it's better than nothing," and he took the bottle.

As Robby shared the snack with Gordo, Vic sat back and watched with appreciation that she had met good men like them in this cruel world full of evil and injustice. Robby committed his life to bring comfort and enjoyment to others. He was one of the most selfless people Vic had ever met. Although Gordo was not as focused on the comfort of others, his heart would not allow him to stand idly by and watch injustice happen. He was a good man to have in your corner when the wolves come to your door. Unfortunately, this time she could not take him with her. She needed him to protect Robby because the wolves knew where he lived. After the fireworks at the beach, she was expecting them to come for revenge. The cartels could not let word get out that they allowed the exchange to be blown without retaliation.

It was only a matter of time before Gregario would come to his senses and send for Alejandra. Vic just hoped she could get to her before they made her disappear. Flying over the changing terrain the minutes dragged by. Vic hoped that the chopper could win the race against Gregario's mental clarity, but she knew it was a long shot. She fully expected her rescue attempt to be met with great resistance.

With only a few minutes before reaching her drop-off location, Vic sent Ivan a message to check in on the other team. She had not heard a status since they took off and Ivan had passed her off to Priya. This made her wonder if the boys were in trouble.

"What's the status of the other team? Did they get out whole?" Vic asked.

"Not yet," replied Ivan. "The boys are taking heavy fire and the Skipper has had to sacrifice his yacht to try to run interference."

"Anyone injured?" Vic probed.

"Chepe took a round, but I have not heard how bad," Ivan reported. "Can't talk now, we're dealing with a Coast Guard issue."

"Understood," replied Vic. "Update me as soon as you can."

Vic knew the risks of going after Robby, they all did, but she couldn't help but feel guilty that her cause was costing Camillo more than her. It was her fault Robby was taken in the first place and there was no way she could've got him back without the help of Camillo's friends. The helicopter leaned as it swung around the ridge. She said a quick prayer for Camillo's team, cleared her head, and prepared to hop out.

CHAPTER 16
HIDE AND HOLD ON

"Get them aboard," commanded The Skipper. "Leave the raft, there's no time."

The crew scurried to get the men aboard. Camilo and Guayo hoisted Chepe as two crewmembers pulled him on deck. With Chepe loaded, the remaining men climbed onto the yacht. Once everyone was on board, The Skipper took over the helm and yelled, "Brace!", as he threw the throttle to all ahead full.

The 20 thousand horsepower superyacht lurched forward, forcing everyone aboard to grasp for something to stabilize themselves. It is very unusual to see a craft of this size move as quickly as it does. The diesel engines growled as the boat sped into the night.

The crew of Coast Guard cutter watched in amazement as the massive yacht surged into motion. They were closing in on the vessel, but not for long. Seeing the boat begin to escape, the crewmen that were topside began firing on them. The cutter adjusted its course to try to cut off the fleeing vessel.

"Do Not fire back!" ordered The Skipper.

He did not want to escalate the situation. Their best course of action was to evade capture. They must outrun the police vessel. Shooting at it would not help them get away.

The passengers and crew all ducked for cover as "The World is Not Enough" quickly increased its distance from the shore and the pursuing ship. The 28-knot top speed of the cutter was no match for the 70-knot max of the superyacht. In ten seconds, they were out of range of the remaining cartel men. Thirty seconds later, the riflemen on the cutter couldn't reach them either. But the danger was not over. They had to disappear into the darkness, but how? The moon was like a spotlight.

With the distance established, The Skipper

turned over the helm and began scanning the radar and various equipment. Apparently, he was struck by an idea because he began dispensing orders to the crew in a rapid-fire manner.

"You men get below and get comfortable; it's going to get a bit bumpy. I'll have my crew take care of your friend."

In the excitement of the escape, no one had noticed that Chepe had bled out. Guayo released the pressure he had been applying and sat back for a moment. The Skipper ordered two of his crew to attend to Chepe and left the men to command the rest of his crew. Camilo and Guayo sat for a moment before they stood up and headed below to the salon where they collapsed into the fine leather couches. Since the crew was busy with the tasks assigned by The Skipper, Camilo decided to help himself to the bar where he grabbed a couple of cold beers, a couple of shot glasses, and a bottle of Cacique from the shelf. Guayo took a beer from Camilo, then watched him pour them each a shot.

"Chepe," Camilo said, raising a shot.

His name was enough. The men toasted their fallen brother, took their shots, and drank their drinks in silence. It was a hell of a day, and they were both lucky to be alive. In fact, if it weren't for

Chepe's cover fire from behind the rocks, someone would be toasting them right now. As the men drank, the tide grew rougher. It was increasingly evident that the day's excitement was not quite over.

To lose the pursuing vessel, The Skipper had plotted a course for a squall a ways off the coast. As they got closer to the storm, they had to reduce their speed quite a bit to adjust to the swells. The yacht raced into the wind and rain as the dark clouds blocked out the light of the moon. The crew had stowed all loose items and prepared the ship for the heavy seas. Waves crashed over the bow as the craft was tossed about. The crew was vigilant as they held fast against the threats of the open ocean.

It was a rough ride, but The Skipper's crew was top-notch. He had invested many hours in these young men, training them to be sailors, but more like sailors on steroids. They could hold their own against human threats as well. These men were in debt to The Skipper and for him they would defend the ship against anything that threatened it. The wind, rain, and stormy seas were what made these men feel alive. To them, rough seas were like riding a bull, except it lasted hours rather than seconds.

Fortunately, this time they only skirted the squall and were traveling as fast as they could in the heavy waves. As they breached the clear skies of the other side, The Skipper used a SATphone to call one of his contacts for help. Through gaps in the clouds, the bright moon reflected off the surface of the waves as The Skipper called in a favor from one of his old CIA buddies. It was going to cost him, but The Skipper was able to get them clear of the coast guard. With the pursuit off, he contacted Ivan.

"Can you get a chopper out here to take these boys home?" The Skipper's tone was down to business.

"No problem, I had one on standby when it sounded like things were heading south," replied Ivan. "You guys made a lot of noise; the dark net feed was full of theories as to what was going on. Send me your coordinates...oh wait, I just got them. Good to see we're on the same page," he continued. The Skipper had pushed send on a message with the coordinates as soon as Ivan said, "No problem". "So, what happened? Is everyone okay?"

"We lost Chepe," reported The Skipper with a somber tone. "Everyone else, present and accounted for."

"Oh, man...sorry to hear that. Let's get him home. You are quite a distance out from the coast. Can you head in and meet between?"

"Yes, I can," answered The Skipper matter-of-factly.

"Plot a course for Playa Nombre de Jesus, Chepe had family there."

"Understood," acknowledged The Skipper. "I'll report to Vic."

"Okay," replied Imri, "but she's taking care of another matter so I'm not sure if she can pick up."

"Another matter," the frustration was clear in The Skipper's voice. "doesn't that girl ever stop stirring up trouble?"

"Actually, it's a bit of a loose end that needs tying up," responded Imri.

"Well, I'll try to reach her anyway. Thanks for sending the chopper." The Skipper's tone softened slightly.

"No problem," said Imri. "Let me know if there's anything else I can help with."

"Roger that," he said as he signed off.

The Skipper took a moment to decompress

before contacting Vic. He looked out at the clear skies in front of him and turned to take in the dark clouds and lightning they had recently emerged from. Breathing in the sea air, he relaxed his shoulders. The wind and the sea were quieting down and the yacht was sailing relatively smoothly toward the Costa Rican coast. The storm had passed, but they did not make it out unscathed.

A crewman approached excitedly, "Skipper, she's taking on water in the starboard cabin and aft storage number two. Louis is plugging the larger hole in the cabin first."

"How bad is it?" asked The Skipper.

"She took a beating sir," the crewman replied. "The bilge pump is running full open and can't keep up. Assuming Louis can plug the holes, we can get to the yard just fine; but she'll need to be repaired soon."

"Aye, we'll drop these boys off and head north." The Skipper acknowledged the crewman's report. "Send word to Jimmy in the shipyard that we're coming and that he'll need to hoist her for repairs. And send word to Rachel at the house that we'll need accommodations for the crew and me." He nodded to dismiss the crewman who returned the nod, turned, and hurried off.

Ever since his retirement, The Skipper had established a network of strategic people to support his lifestyle. The primary factor was always privacy, his team needed to keep their mouths shut. Jimmy was the best boatman on the Pacific coast. From raft to aircraft carrier, he could fix it all. He was the one who had installed the Phalanx system. The Skipper met Rachel at the Coos Bay Speedway where he liked to feed his need for speed. Her 1967 Shelby Mustang GT500 Super Snake nearly inched out his 1968 Yenko Camaro RS/SS. That was the beginning of a rivalry and friendship that has lasted nearly two decades. Rachel had inherited an estate that overlooked Haynes Slough and disappeared into the forest to the west. There was a main house with ten small cabins that spread into the woods about five acres. Since The Skipper wasn't a fan of crowds, when he wasn't with his crew on the open sea, he chose to be a recluse in the forest. Fortunately, it was only a short boat ride from the shipyard.

The Skipper set his eyes on the horizon and took a moment to quiet his mind so he could focus. The firefight had opened his adrenal glands and he was still pretty keyed up. His eyes examined the area where the moon reflected off the water as it peered through a crack in the clouds. He then shifted his gaze to the dark luminous clouds that appeared to be trying to flank them to the port side. Settling on the course for the coast just out of sight in front of them, The Skipper ruminated the current sit rep. He took a last look around before heading to his cabin to call Vic.

Closing the door behind him, The Skipper stepped into the luxurious master cabin. Kicking off his shoes he staged them at the door. His toes curled and grabbed at the carpet which helped him relax. He always took it hard when the team didn't make it back whole, even if they weren't his men directly. He was The Skipper, and he felt accountable for the successes and failures of every mission.

As he reclined on the bed, he leaned over and pulled a Miller Genuine Draft from the bottom drawer of the nightstand. This was another one of the customizations that Jimmy had provided, the bottom drawer was retrofitted to be refrigerated. Twisting off the cap, he took a long swig and picked up the phone to dial Vic.

"What's up Skip?" Vic answered in a hushed voice on the second ring.

"Sit Rep," The Skipper's tone sounded as if he

was reporting to the panel at the Pentagon. "We have a casualty. Chepe didn't make it."

"Oh, man," The news was not unexpected but that didn't remove the sting. "How's Camilo?"

"Last I saw he and Guayo are working on a bottle of Cacique and washing it down with cervezas," he replied.

"Sounds about right," Vic said. "What else?"

"My boat took it pretty hard..."

"Yeah, what the fuck was that?" Vic interrupted. "You lit up the beach like an Independence Day celebration."

"Yeah, sorry about that," The Skipper answered less than apologetically. "Those boat crews were closing on your boys, and I didn't see any other way to keep them from getting wiped out in a matter of seconds. They were going to be in the crossfire of insurmountable forces."

"I get it," Vic approved, "I just had no idea you had those capabilities."

"You know me," he said slyly, "I don't like to show my full hand unless forced." The Skipper was always proud of his toys and even though he loved surprises, it was hard for him not to show them off the first chance he got.

"Anyway," The Skipper continued, "Ivan has a

bird headed our way to pick these boys up and take them inland. Once they debark, we're heading north for repairs. So don't call me if you get yourself into more shit. I won't have any way to help." His gruff attitude was partial saltiness from years of militant operations but mostly it was simply his natural personality. Those that knew him understood that it was just the way he was, and he didn't mean anything by it.

"No problem, buddy," Vic whispered. "I'm sorry we broke your yacht."

"I'll send you the bill," The Skipper retorted, half kidding. "Don't forget, you still owe me, and don't think those two floozies make up for it."

"Who, Ashley and Jennifer?" Vic asked coyly. "They were a gift, Skippy. I know how grumpy you get with all those lonely days at sea."

"Next time, bring three," The Skipper countered. "Unless you want to join…"

"In your dreams, big guy," she shut him down quick. "Thanks for the update, I gotta' go."

"Roger, watch your six." The Skipper signed off.

CHAPTER 17
CANINES AND CORRIDORS

Tucking her phone back into her pocket, Vic slid through the shadows as she approached the fence. The hike from the drop zone was an uphill push through the secondary forest. It wasn't thick, but there was plenty of brush to hide her approach. Although it was not a full-grown forest, the area was not without its share of threats. There were several venomous insects and reptiles to watch out for along with various other predators.

The wind turbines in the North were positioned to pick up the breeze from the west. The night air carried the aroma of a fragrant Royal Poinciana tree and manure. With the wind at her face, the dogs were upwind and had not picked up her scent. Now that she was close, it was only a matter of time before they clued in on her.

She pulled the chicken snacks from her pocket and put a couple in each hand. It was a good thing she did because before she knew it, she was face to face with a couple of mean-looking Costa Rican mutts. In the shadows of the trees that lined the property, the dog's patchy coats of brown, black, and white camouflaged them. They snarled and growled a low warning when they caught her scent, but once they knew her location, they began the full alarm.

It's not unusual for farm dogs to bark. There is a lot of wildlife surrounding the property and they chase off unwanted intruders nightly. The guards were accustomed to them getting excited about something, so they usually ignored them unless they didn't stop for some time. Vic had to get them to quiet down in a hurry to keep the guards from getting suspicious.

Using her soft "dog whisperer" voice, Vic began to sing the lyrics to the last song she'd heard. "Despacito Quiero respirar tu cuello..." Perhaps the beasts were Luis Fonsi fans because the singing began to work. The guard dogs turned their heads curiously and listened as they relaxed their barks.

With extreme caution, Vic slowly raised and reached out her arms to present her peace offerings. She'd never seen a dog turn down a snack and again she was not disappointed when she was able to bribe the nice puppies with snacks. The ferocious beasts became tame with the help of some chicken and a little sedative. She sang softly to them until their eyes rolled back and they laid down for a nap.

She let out a sigh of relief that she was able to terminate the canines. She considered herself a bit of a dog lover even though she didn't have one of her own. Her lifestyle was unconducive to caring for pets. But once her mission was complete and Gregario was dead, she fully expected to get a Doberman Pinscher puppy.

With the dog threat handled, Vic watched from behind the tree for her opportunity to cross the open field unseen. She had to time her exposure to the guards at the front and the back of the building. They seemed to wander back and forth a bit, but they had developed a sort of natural rhythm to their wandering. When the guard at the rear turned back around the corner she launched from her position and raced to the wall. With her back to the wall, she slid to the corner in pursuit of the rear guard.

Careful to silence her footsteps she slid along the wall following the guard at a short distance. The farmhouse was basically a rectangle with a porch attached to the long front. With the exception of a quick peek inside the back door, the guard kept his focus in front of him and occasionally the field to his right. Vic did her best to stay in the shadows on the left under the eaves. Once she reached the door, she ducked inside behind a counter.

During her hike in, Priya had sent over floor plans with the heat signatures within the house. The room she entered was a kind of mudroom space that was unoccupied. There were halls that crossed the house front to back and side to side dividing the sections evenly and converging in the dining area. The kitchen and bathroom flanked the front entrance and rows of even size rooms spread from the dining area to the perimeter of the house. There was an open door to a staircase next to the bathroom.

Peering around the edge of the cabinet, Vic watched as people crossed back and forth through the dining room. Crossing that room undetected would be a challenge to say the least. She had no idea which room Alejandra was in. If she simply went door to door, she risked the person in that room being a cartel member or someone who would announce her presence and she would have to deal with the guards who responded. Neither situation allowed for a simple in and out.

The longer she stayed put, the greater the risk of being discovered. She needed to move. She noticed a breaker box on the wall. "That may help," she thought to herself. Turning her attention back to the vista to the front door, she caught another break she desperately needed. Alejandra stepped out from the kitchen with dirty kitchen rags in hand. She crossed the hall and front door and took the staircase to the basement.

Seizing the opportunity, Vic sprang up and opened the breaker panel. She flipped the switches to every breaker in the box and the house went dark. Without hesitation, she followed the corners down the hall into the dining room. Finding the table in the center of the room, she made her way around the chairs toward the stairs.

The guards began shouting back and forth to each other yelling for someone to check the breakers. The power grid in Costa Rica is less than reliable and quick blackouts are common. In the older houses, when the power comes back on, it often trips the breakers. The guards assumed this was the case so they did not see cause for alarm.

As she was passing the hall, one of the guards who was yelling about the breaker box stumbled into the room. Vic did not have time to avoid him as he charged forward with outstretched arms. As soon as he touched her shoulder Vic reacted. She reached up and grabbed his wrist pulling him forward. The force caused him to slam his head on the edge of the table with a loud thud, knocking him out. Vic hurriedly scrambled out of the room and to the stairway. As she descended the stairs she whispered, "Alejandra?" A few more steps and she called out again. This time she got a quizzical response.

"Si?" Alejandra recognized the voice but could not place it.

"Pura Vida Mae, it's Victoria from the ship," Vic used the secret phrase she had asked Alejandra to pass on to the kids that were being trafficked. "I have to get you out of here, you are in danger."

"What?" Alejandra's brain was trying to comprehend what was happening.

"Take my hand, let's go," Vic commanded gently but assertively.

Recognizing who Vic was, Alejandra obeyed and followed her down to the basement. Vic led blindly down the hall until Alejandra pulled her back and said, "This way."

They entered a room next to the stairs that smelled of bleach and detergent. Vic realized it was the laundry room as the lights came back on. "That was fast," she thought.

"We have to get back upstairs so we can get out of here," Vic said.

"There's another way," Alejandra replied.

"How?" Vic asked puzzled. "The front and back doors are upstairs."

"There's a tunnel to another door at the end of the hall," answered Alejandra.

"Is it guarded?" Vic asked.

"There might be one or two guards at the door, but there are more upstairs."

"Okay, let's go," said Vic. Not wanting to waste time, she stepped toward the door.

"Wait," said Alejandra pulling her back. "The guards will check all the rooms, we'll be caught. You need to hide here." She picked up a stack of clean sheets, unfolded them, and piled them on the floor. The sound of boots coming down the stairs told Vic she should listen to Alejandra. She laid down on the pile of sheets and Alejandra quickly threw some on top of her. She quickly started the washing machine and began to measure detergent. A moment later, a guard popped his head in and asked what she was doing.

Vic prepared herself for attack should he find her. Without panic, Alejandra simply raised the measuring cup and detergent and shot him a look. Understanding it was a stupid question and she was obviously doing laundry, he snapped back, "Hazlo." Having re-established his authority and completing his check of the area, he continued to the next room.

Once clear, Alejandra lifted the sheets off of Vic and helped her up. She held her finger in front of her lips indicating that she wanted Vic to stay quiet. She leaned out and looked down the hall. Once the guard stepped into the next room, she motioned for Vic to follow her. The pair raced quickly and quietly to the door at the end of the opposite hall. Alejandra opened the door, the pair stepped through, and she closed it quietly behind Vic.

The tunnel was dark with only the light from

the cracks around the door providing light. "What is this place?" whispered Vic.

"It's a tunnel but I don't know where to," Alejandra whispered back. "A couple of years ago, some of the boys were sent here and would return very dirty. Some of them never came back and the others refused to talk about them. I assume they were being used to dig this tunnel and others. Sometimes I am asked to bring food to the guards at the door."

The women slowly crept down the dark tunnel using the wall for guidance. Vic led with her right hand grasping the handle of her Adamas knife and the other holding Alejandra's. Their eyes slowly adjusted to the dim light from the door behind them. Twenty meters in front of them, the tunnel curved out of sight to the right and they could not see beyond the bend.

"The door is just around there," whispered Alejandra as she pointed in front of them. "There is probably a guard there."

The tunnel smelled of damp earth and the air was cool and moist. It was not much wider than the door they came through but was opening up the deeper they progressed. The women tread softly on the dirt floor to minimize the sounds of their footprints. Step by step they approached the bend where a new light source began to illuminate the area ahead of them.

Vic held up her hand to indicate she wanted Alejandra to stay where she was and not move. Alejandra pulled her body back against the wall and froze. Releasing Alejandra's hand, Vic moved her hand to the grip of her pistol and slowly bent forward to peer around the corner. Keeping her head close to the wall she tried to remain unseen as she searched for the light source. About ten meters ahead was a guard leaning back against the wall playing on his phone. The light from the screen created a glow that cast down the corridor.

The light followed the tunnel past the guard illuminating a split. The tunnel continued around another bend to the right but shot off to the left just beyond the guard. Vic quickly ran through her options. It would be nearly impossible to close the distance to the guard undetected. If she fired her weapon, it would definitely give away her presence and their location. As she was considering her options, the guard's phone rang.

He answered it and without looking up took a couple of steps in their direction. Vic tightened her grip on her weapons and prepared to strike. "¿Los perros? No sé," he said as he turned around and took the passage to his left. Apparently, someone was having trouble locating the dogs and wanted the guard to see if they were around. Vic heard a door open and shut and they were left in darkness.

She used her watch to create a small light and turned back to look at Alejandra.

"That's the door out," whispered Alejandra with great concern.

"Where does the tunnel lead?" asked Vic. "Is there another exit?"

"I don't know," Alejandra replied. "I have never been past the door, It was forbidden."

"The guard could be right outside," I think our best option is to see where the tunnel leads and hope for another way out," Vic recommended.

Alejandra nodded her understanding and Vic reached out for her hand to help calm her as she guided her into the darkness. They walked quickly and quietly past the corridor outside and followed the bend of the tunnel. As her eyes continued to adjust to the darkness, Vic could see further down the tunnel. There was another door about fifty meters ahead. There was a low hum coming from that direction that grew louder as they approached.

CHAPTER 18

THAT'S A LOT OF HARDWARE

Outside the door, Vic's left hand released Alejandra's and pulled her Sig P365 from its holster. She put her right hand on the double door and felt the vibration of machines on the other side. She slowly turned the doorknob and pulled the door open a crack to peer through. The bright fluorescent lights were blinding, and it took her eyes a moment to adjust to the light. Cool air rushed across her face as she leaned in to look through the slit. She was able to see large cabinets of computer servers.

She motioned to Alejandra to stay put against the wall. Taking a deep breath, she pulled the door open and slid inside. As the door closed behind her, she placed her right hand back on her Adamas knife and proceeded down the aisle between rows of servers. Her eyes scanned the room looking for threats as her mind tried to assess where she had just stumbled into.

The room of servers was massive. She counted twelve rows, each about a futball field in length. Concrete pillars supported the ceiling every twenty meters and had cable chases mounted to them. The cables disappeared behind a drop ceiling. The white tile floor was pristine, with no trace of dust or dirt from the tunnel outside.

The contrast of this space to the rundown farmhouse was dramatic. The musty farmhouse smelled thick of farm animals and body odor. In contrast, the air of this room carried an aroma of performance electronics and the sweet smell of freon from the air conditioners. The muggy humid air was swapped for cool dry freshness.

As she made her way to the far end of the row, she leaned forward and peeped around the corner to the right. There was a terminal in the center of the wall a couple of rows down that separated the large banks of servers that lined the perimeter of the room. Turning her head to the left, the servers ended just short of a wall of plastic sheeting. Apparently, there were expansion plans in progress.

Through the plastic, she could see the halo of construction lights and there were blurry images of wheelbarrows with shovel handles sticking out, lined up against the temporary wall. A door had been roughed in to allow access to the area without an open seam that would allow the construction dust to flow into the server room. The door was directly visible from the terminal. There was no way out that door without being seen.

Why was this server room buried underground in Costa Rica? What was the cartel doing with all that processing power? Vic tried to hail Ivan on the coms, "Ivan, can you hear me?" she whispered. There was no response. She tried again, "Ivan, come in." Still nothing. Vic was unclear whether it was the subterranean room or a jammer of some kind that was blocking the signal. Either way, she was on her own.

Keeping her guard and watching for threats, she made her way to the terminal. As she pressed the keys to wake the interface, she recalled her first encounter with Ivan. That day at the coffee shop in Moscow, she learned just how limited her hacking skills were. She would still be there trying to hack into the Bank of Moscow's system if the nosy college kid hadn't been looking over her shoulder. Ivan had shared some tips with her over the years since then, but she was still a rookie when it came to accessing systems. Fortunately, the cartel was relying primarily on the secrecy of the location and the guards outside to prevent access to their system. After all, who would be ballsy enough to try to infiltrate their farmhouse and gain access to the terminal? Their greatest threats were from others hacking into the system remotely.

As Vic accessed the system, the reports of firewall and brute force protection were evident, but she was unable to determine the purpose of the servers and what they were processing. She used a few tricks Ivan had shown her to connect to a remote system using SSH. A few keystrokes later and Ivan had access to the terminal.

Just as the confirmation of connection was displayed on the screen, Vic heard noise from beyond the plastic. Someone was coming. She quickly backed out of the system and withdrew down the nearest aisle of servers. She heard the door on the plastic wall open, someone wipe their feet, and the door shut. A man began whistling a tune as he walked toward the terminal. Random things often click in Victoria's mind, and this was another of those occasions. She immediately recognized the tune, it was "Whistle" by Flo Rida. Not really a song she liked, but it had a way of getting stuck in her head whenever she heard it. She couldn't stop her mind from singing along. It made for an interesting soundtrack to the moment.

She listened as he sat down and began typing, not missing a note as he continued whistling. Vic used the reflection off the glass of the cabinet across from her to peer around the corner and get a glimpse of the whistling man. She did not recognize him, but he did not appear to be one of the kids from the farmhouse. He was well dressed in khaki pants and a bright blue short-sleeve button-down. His hair was styled, and his cowboy boots were shined. Head to toe he was well put together. His attention to his appearance reminded Vic of Leo. The reflection wasn't perfect, so it was hard to make out the man's face and it was impossible to see what was on the monitor.

The whistling stopped abruptly, and Vic ducked back beyond the view of the reflection. Something on the screen had grabbed the man's attention. There was little more intel Vic could gather at this point, so she thought it best to use the man's focus on the computer to distract him from her exit.

Making her way to the door where she had left Alejandra, she slipped through and silently secured the door behind her. Alejandra let out a small gasp as the door opened but relaxed when she saw that it was Vic and not one of the guards.

"Is there a way out?" she whispered.

"Not without being noticed," replied Vic.

"What's in there?" asked Alejandra curiously.

"It's a server room with a lot of computers," Victoria answered. "Someone was coming so I had to get out before we were discovered. Let's see if we can slip out past the guard at the door. Maybe we'll get lucky, and he will be out looking for the dogs."

Alejandra nodded and reached out her hand. Vic holstered her pistol, took Alejandra's hand, and crept through the dark tunnel back toward the door. Coming from the illuminated server room, Vic's eyes gradually adjusted back to the darkness of the tunnel, but she had poor visibility. Her right hand alternated between feeling her way along the wall and grasping the handle of her knife. As she ran her fingers across the wall in front of her, she felt a corner. They had made it to the door unseen.

Vic released Alejandra's hand and drew her pistol.

"Stay behind me and follow me close!" Vic commanded.

"Sí, claro." Alejandra understood Vic's sharpness.

Vic slowly turned the handle on the door to open it. It began to squeak so she quickly threw it open and stepped out. The humid tropical night air was profuse. In front of her were steps carved in the dirt that led to the surface. Vic held her pistol at the ready and grasped her knife as she climbed the steps and surveyed the area. The entrance was covered by a massive Guanacaste tree. A dirt path ran from the driveway of the farmhouse past the tree and followed the fence line into a patch of trees in the direction of the wind farm.

The night sky was blanketed with tropical clouds pregnant with moisture. It would not take much for the building pressure between them to cause them to burst and release a downpour. The steady breeze pressed on them as it herded the vapors. The moon was barely visible through one thin spot in the clouds. The stars were completely blacked out. It was a very dark night.

Vic pulled Alejandra to the base of the tree where they huddled in the shadows. Under the porchlight, Vic could see the guard at the back door keeping watch over his zone. Under the tree's cover, the guard could not see them. But, if they tried to run across the field to the trees they would most likely be spotted.

As the guard was about to reach the corner of the house, the one that was guarding the door to the tunnel appeared on the far end of the porch carrying one of the dogs. He yelled something at the back door guard as he handed him the dog and pointed toward the fence where Vic had fed them the snacks with sedatives. After completing his report and telling the other guard what to do, he stepped off the porch and started to return to his post at the door.

"We've got to move," Vic whispered. "Do not stand up! We must get to the trees."

Alejandra turned to look in the direction of the trees with a look of despair. The trees were a long way off and it would take a long time to get there. She knew better than to question. She simply nodded and followed Vic as she crouched and moved quickly through the tall grass. As they created some space, they became more exposed. Vic dropped and slithered on her belly through the grass and brush slowly to avoid rustling the bushes enough to attract attention. Alejandra mimicked Vic's movements quite well for not having been trained. It was as if she intuitively understood the caution needed to survive.

It was counter-intuitive to "runaway" by crawling on your belly. Every instinct inside says to get away as fast as you can. Crawling makes you feel like you are just asking to be caught. However, by moving slowly and avoiding detection, the women were able to slip away without being discovered. If they made a break for it, their movements would alert the guards and they would be captured or killed.

Slipping into the cover of the trees, the women heard the guards yelling and could see them shining their flashlights out into the fields. They froze in position and listened intently. They could make out the men calling for Alejandra. It was clear that Gregario had contacted them. Vic had got to her just in time. Now they needed to get some distance between them and find some transportation. It would be a tough hike through the forest, but they needed to move, or the men would find them.

The adrenaline racing through Alejandra as she made her escape enabled her to nearly keep up with Vic's lead. Vic raced through the trees following the paths of the local wildlife. Her training had taught her to look for trails like these to be able to move quickly through the thick brush. Quite often, trails like these would lead to water sources which would generally lead to people. Vic hoped to find a stream that was feeding another farmer who would have a car or truck she could "borrow".

Now that she was above ground, she attempted to use her coms.

"Ivan, do you copy?" She hailed.

"I'm here Vic," Ivan replied. "What's going on?"

"I've got Alejandra. We need immediate evac!" Vic answered. "Do you have my coordinates?"

"Yes, I've got your location. I'll send help." Ivan affirmed. "But it's going to take some time. The helicopter is refueling."

The women could hear the men hollering as they searched in their direction. Fear shone in Alejandra's face and Victoria tried to reassure her with a gentle smile. She turned away and whispered harshly, "We don't have time."

CHAPTER 19

TIGHTEN YOUR GRIP AND LEAN IN

"We have to stay on the move," Vic said as she started back down the trail away from the men.

"Yes, I can see the men approaching through infrared from the satellite," Ivan agreed. "There is a heat signature of some small structure southeast of you. Continue in that direction and I'll try to help lead you out."

"Thanks, Ivan," said Vic. "Keep me updated."

"Of course, M'lady," Ivan said, trying to lighten the tension of the moment. "Once you get wheels, I'll direct you to an LZ. I'll have Priya help track your pursuers."

"Good idea," Vic said. She had become impressed with Priya's contributions to the team ever since Ivan recommended bringing her on board.

Alejandra held tightly to Vic's hand as she dragged her through the brush and vines. Their pace was making some distance from the men, but not enough. They might need some time to access and hotwire a vehicle. Alejandra was going as fast as she could, but Vic was a master at traversing the jungle.

"Look," said Alejandra out of breath. She pointed over Vic's left shoulder.

In the dark distance, Vic's eyes began to make out a shack through the trees. Vic slowed the pace and adjusted their course for the structure. She put her finger in front of her mouth to instruct Alejandra to stay quiet as she searched the structure for occupants and transportation options.

Moving in close, she peered through the corner of a window. The slight breeze blew the corner of the curtains back just enough for Vic to get a glimpse of a man passed out on a couch with a Pilsen in his hand. The table next to him littered with empties and food wrappers. This was a pretty standard living for a lot of these guys. They worked hard labor for little pay and spent their money on beer or liquor. A guy like this, living in these woods definitely rides a dirt bike. But where did he park it?

A common problem with using the kickstand to park a motorcycle in the jungle was that the rains made the dirt soft. You could put your kickstand down and walk away, but when you returned, the stand will have sunk into the mud and your bike will be laying on its side. An easy fix in places like this was to simply lean it against a tree.

The women cautiously circled the cabina looking for a road. Around the second corner, Vic discovered tire trails leading through the trees away from the house. It was not really a driveway, more like an end to a trail. Along one of the tire trails, Vic spotted a red and yellow moto leaning against a cedar tree facing them.

"Follow me," instructed Vic. "Stay in the trees. I'm going to push the bike out of range before I try to start it."

She grabbed the handlebars and pushed. It was in neutral, so she continued turning the bike around. Once headed away from the house, Vic intensified her pace and jogged the moto a hundred meters from the shack. With a safe distance and the cover of rain, Vic quickly traced the wires for the ignition and used her knife to cut and strip them. Once rewired, Vic swung out the kickstart and jumped on the lever. The engine rumbled but didn't start. She tried again, and again. The fourth attempt and the moto bawled to life.

The sound of the engine starting aroused the sleeping man who yelled and quickly appeared in the doorway of the cabina.

"Get on," Vic yelled over the engine.

Alejandra sprang from the trees, threw her leg over the seat behind Vic, and tucked her skirt up under her legs. This wasn't her first time on the back of a bike. Alejandra's arms tightened around Vic's waist as she twisted the throttle. Braaaap, the bike lunged forward. The man threw his beer bottle at them, but it wasn't even close to reaching them. The women raced away as the man pursued them down the path a few meters before giving up.

"Ivan, we're on the move," Vic said into her coms.

"I'm tracking you now," replied Ivan. "Priya is online as well and ready to assist."

"The men from the farmhouse are now searching in vehicles," Priya inserted herself. "The nearest one is north of you, approaching at about forty kilometers per hour. The others are heading away from you."

"It would appear they still do not know what happened to Alejandra," Ivan chimed back in. "The helicopter is 14 minutes from the LZ and you should arrive at about that time as well. I sent the coordinates to your phone in case we lose coms; however, I will lead you there. You should reach a dirt road in about 125 meters. Turn right and take the road south."

"Copy that," replied Vic.

Sensing Alejandra was relatively comfortable on the back of the motorcycle, Vic took the corners with increasing intensity. Alejandra held tight and leaned perfectly to allow the proper angle to take the tight turns at high speeds. Gravel was tossed from the knobby tires as the two sped through the warm tropical air.

"The men that were going in your direction have turned off," announced Priya. "You can relax."

"I'll relax when I get her to the safe house," replied Vic. "But I'll slow down so we don't draw attention."

Vic turned her head to speak to Alejandra. "You're safe now."

"Are you sure?" Alejandra asked.

"Yes," Vic tried to assure her. "They turned away from us back there. My friends are tracking them from the sky."

"You have very special friends," Alejandra said emphatically.

"Yes, yes I do," Vic said with pride.

As Vic eased up on the throttle and the motorcycle reached a reasonable speed, Alejandra loosened her hold around Vic's waist. She still held on, but it was more like a couple of girls out for a ride to the bar than women fleeing.

The rest of the ride to the LZ was a nice chance for Alejandra's mind to begin to process what had just happened. She thought about the others she left behind. It wasn't her intention, but she had become the only kind person whom many of them were allowed to interact with. She felt guilty for leaving them behind. She even took a moment to consider what it was going to be like to see her daughter Cynthia again. What would she say to her?

Vic spent the time trying to ensure there weren't any loose ends she was missing. Although not perfect, things were going well for the most part. She didn't want to lose the momentum they were building.

Ivan directed Vic to the parking lot of a chicken processing plant on the outskirts of one of the larger towns in the area. The women arrived a few minutes before the helicopter. The place seemed vacant, but Vic didn't want to take any chances. She stashed the bike in the bushes and led Alejandra to a wall on the loading docks that shielded them from view from the road and lot in front of the factory. Vic would peer out and check the area was clear every few moments.

"They are close," updated Ivan. "You should see them any minute."

"We're on the loading docks on the east side," Vic reported.

"Copy that, I'll let the pilot know," Ivan confirmed.

"Please make arrangements to get that moto back to its owner," Vic said. "Make sure he's compensated for us "borrowing" it.'

"You got it, Vic," Ivan replied.

It was only a couple of minutes wait, but it seemed like much longer before the women heard the propellers in the distance. Alejandra spotted a small white light far in the distance in the direction of the sound. She pointed and Vic nodded in acknowledgment. They watched as the light grew bigger until the chopper spun and set down between tall lights that illuminated the lot.

"Let's go," said Vic as she took Alejandra's hand and led her to the helicopter.

The ladies climbed in and as soon as Vic strapped Alejandra in she hollered at the pilot.

"Get us in the air."

He immediately pulled the stick and the chopper lifted off. Alejandra's eyes grew wide with excitement. She wasn't sure if she was scared or exhilarated. She had flown on large passenger jets six times but never anything like this. Her organs floated in her torso as the helicopter banked and spun pushing her up, down, and side to side. It was better than the carnival rides when the fiesta came to town. Her day just kept getting better.

Vic leaned her head back against the bulkhead and watched the smile grow on Alejandra's face. It was rewarding to see her joy. Vic knew she had witnessed unspeakable acts at the hands of the cartel. She knew that Alejandra's life was not usually one of joy but rather of fear and sorrow. But at that moment, none of that seemed to matter to Alejandra. She was having a good time and that was fun to watch.

While watching Alejandra, Vic's mind drifted to the computer server room. What was the Gulf Cartel doing with all that tech? That wasn't their normal method of operation. They were more brute force and fear than intelligent crimes. And that guy at the keyboard, he didn't look like one of the Gulf thugs. There had to be a connection to the Central American Cartel.

That place was so clean and sterile. Everything in the room was new and professionally installed. It was a great contrast to the dirty farmhouse with its odor of human filth and smoke. Vic didn't know much about that kind of tech, but the hardware looked pretty state-of-the-art to her. She hoped Ivan would have some answers when they spoke next. For now, she needed to get Alejandra to the safe house.

After about ten minutes in the air, Alejandra realized that she had no idea where they were going. The thrill of the ride had captured her attention and she hadn't considered what the next step was.

"Where are we going?" Alejandra yelled over

the sound of the rotors slapping and the jet engines screaming.

"A safe place," Vic hollered back. "We need to make sure they don't know where you are and that your family is safe. I have a home that you will stay at until we know it is safe for you to return to your family. We'll talk more when we land."

"How much longer?" Alejandra asked.

"Only a few more minutes," Vic answered

Alejandra returned her attention to the scenery whizzing by outside the open door. The light of distant villages looked like fireflies on the horizon. Her mind flipped between thoughts of how amazing the ride was and what was going to happen next. She was enjoying the flight, but her anxiety was rising the closer they got to the end of the ride.

Vic's phone vibrated in her pocket, and she pulled it to check the notification. Ivan had sent transportation arrangements and coordinates. He had arranged for a car to be at the landing zone, a Toyota 4Runner. In the truck would be a go bag with two sets of credit cards and IDs, as well as a pair of keys to the safe house. Ivan had arranged for the safe house to be stocked with food and some weapons that Vic always requested and plenty of ammo.

Alejandra let out a small squeal as her stomach dropped. The pilot had taken an aggressive approach to the landing but set the helicopter down so gently it took a moment to confirm they were on the ground.

"That's our ride," Vic said, pointing to the 4Runner.

Alejandra took her hand and Vic led her to the vehicle. Walking hand in hand had become the norm. It was Vic's way of reassuring Alejandra as she led her. The security of Vic's grip helped calm Alejandra's nerves as she faced each new experience. It was the physical semblance of Vic's expression of "I've got you," and Alejandra's confirmation of "I trust you."

The girls climbed into the truck and began their road trip to the safe house.

"Okay, since I'm driving you get to be DJ," Vic said with a smile.

"Oh...I don't know, what do you like to hear?" Alejandra said hesitantly. It had been a long time since she had a choice in anything.

"You can search the radio for something you

like," said Victoria. "When you find a song you like, just leave the dial there."

Alejandra scanned the dial until an upbeat song came bouncing through the speakers.

"Soy yo (soy, soy, soy, soy, soy, soy, soy)..." the singer sang the Spanish words "It's me" with confidence.

"Do you know this one?" Victoria asked.

"No, but it sounds fun," Alejandra answered with a smile.

"This is Soy Yo by Bomba Estéreo," said Victoria. "I really like it and it's easy to learn."

The women bounced their heads and sang along. Vic thought this was a great song of empowerment for Alejandra. She decided she would make a playlist for Alejandra that included songs like this. Songs that would help her find the woman that she wanted to be. For the past several years she had been told who the cartel wanted her to be. Now it was time for her to decide for herself.

CHAPTER 20
BUILDING BONDS

"Tomorrow, we will go shopping for clothes." Victoria was showing Alejandra around the safe house. The small house had two bedrooms, a shared bathroom, and a living room. The simple kitchen was clean and stocked. They had all the cookware and ingredients they would need to prepare meals. The cupboards were full of beans, rice, and other dry goods. There was a fruit basket on the table with fresh bananas, mangos, and mamon chinos. Alejandra opened the refrigerator and grinned, it was full of beautiful vegetables and juices and some chicken. She was not used to having this many options to cook. She was used to preparing meals with reduced produce and whatever were the cheapest ingredients that the cartel men could find.

"What would you like me to make you?" Alejandra assumed her standard submissive role. She expected it was her place to serve Vic.

"What?" Vic noticed Alejandra's mannerisms and didn't waste any time correcting her. "We are equals. I need your help as much as you need mine."

Alejandra looked at Victoria quizzically. Her mind was trying to understand what Victoria was saying. She had overheard a cartel guard talking about what she had done to the Serbians. She also heard about the kids that were sent home with money for a fresh start. She witnessed Vic sneak her out of the farmhouse and race into the night on a stolen motorcycle. The woman in front of her was a superhero, how could she possibly say they are equal?

"I don't understand," Alejandra's face expressed her confusion.

"Well," Victoria started. "I needed you to deliver a message to those kids in order to be able to save them. You needed my help to escape Gregorio and the Gulf Cartel. Now I need your help again."

"How could I possibly be helpful to you?" Alejandra was at a loss. "You can do everything."

"I need you to tell me everything you can think of about the people that you have met since they took you. That includes others that were taken."

"I don't know where to start," said Alejandra. "I don't know what you want to hear, and I have met so many people, most of them kidnapped like me."

"Don't worry about it," Victoria reassured her. "We have time. Whenever you think of something you can share it. No rush. For now, let's just get some food and get some rest."

"So...do you want me to make us something?" Alejandra still wasn't getting it.

"How about we cook together," Victoria suggested.

"I would like that," Alejandra said with a smile.

"I tell you what, why don't you take a shower, and we'll cook after we get cleaned up," Victoria suggested.

"Sounds perfect." Alejandra agreed.

Once they had freshened up, the women made a traditional casado of rice, black beans, plantains, salad, a tortilla, and chicken. Ivan had even arranged for a bottle of Cacique to be in the room. Victoria took the opportunity to create her favorite guaro drink of Cacique and Tang. It was simple, strong, and hit the spot. Alejandra gave it a try and although she didn't have Victoria's appreciation of the concoction, she drank a bit more than she expected. It was starting to get late but both ladies were running high on adrenaline and were more wired than exhausted.

The ladies danced to reggaeton music as they cleaned up dinner. It was a drastic contrast to the way the day started for either of them. Alejandra used the leftover rice and beans to prepare gallo pinto for breakfast and placed it in the refrigerator. With the kitchen cleaned, they headed to the living room with their drinks. Alejandra told Victoria how much she enjoyed the helicopter ride. The girls took turns recounting the highlights of Alejandra's great escape.

Vic sent a quick message to Ivan to ask him to set up a debriefing with the team in the morning.

"Good to hear you made it safe," Ivan replied. "So far it looks like they have no idea where Alejandra is or how she got out. I'll send the team invites and login instructions. See you in the morning."

Victoria knew that she was going to ask a lot from Alejandra. It was not going to be easy for her to talk about her experiences. Victoria decided to share some of her own to gain a little credit.

"Would you like to hear about how our paths crossed?" Victoria asked.

"Um...sure." Alejandra was caught a bit off guard by the question.

"It all started many years ago on a sunny day at the beach..." Victoria began the story of the day Richie was killed and she witnessed Gregario loading Alejandra into a box truck and driving away.

Although it was painful for Alejandra to hear Victoria's version of the story of the day she was taken, it helped her to understand why Vic was helping her get away from her captors. Alejandra struggled to imagine Vic as a vulnerable teenager. She seemed so strong and confident. She was obviously able to handle herself. Vic was smart and tough. Imagining her crying and helpless, holding her cousin as he slipped away was hard to envision.

Victoria did not share the whole story that brought her to this point, just what started her quest. She didn't like to talk about herself. It wasn't that she was embarrassed or ashamed of her past; she was quite proud of the woman she had become. Victoria simply did not like to be the center of attention. As she concluded her story, Alejandra asked about her life before that day.

"Did you grow up in Guanacaste?" she asked.

"Yes, my family is scattered along the coast from Playa Flamingo to Santa Teresa," Victoria answered. "I spent most of my childhood between Playa Flamingo and Playa Negra. My mother was a housekeeper and worked for resorts until she was able to get some private clients and picked up side jobs for vacation rentals. I didn't see my father often. He was a surf instructor and would travel up and down the coast."

"Did you ever eat at the restaurant I worked at?" Alejandra asked.

"Sure," replied Victoria. "I really like the patacones and frijoles. They are very crispy. And I knew Maria that took the orders."

"Oh, Maria," Alejandra said with a smile as she remembered her coworker from long ago. "She was a sweet girl. Do you know if she is still there?"

"I haven't been back there since Richie died," answered Victoria. "I don't know if she still works there or if the restaurant is even still open."

"I can't imagine Senora Flor letting the restaurant close," said Alejandra. "It has been in the family for years and her daughter Andrea was set to take over. I assume she would be in charge now, Senora Flor must be close to ninety years old."

The women spent another half hour talking about mutual people they knew before calling it a night and heading to bed. It was good that Victoria had opened up and shared about her young life. It had helped Alejandra remember the world outside of the cartel and helped her to know and trust Victoria more. Knowing that Victoria had grown up much like she had made a small part of her, way deep inside, think that there might be a chance for her to be a strong confident woman someday.

She was surprised to learn that Victoria was a normal girl that had taken her pain and loss and harnessed it into strength and skills. So many people use adversity as an excuse to give up or not be able to handle life. Victoria had chosen not to give in to the easy road of letting herself be broken and weak. She overcame her situation and learned to be a force. That is what Alejandra hoped for, to be a strong woman who did not let her circumstances define who she was but rather face them with confidence and a strong will like Vic.

Lying in her bed, Alejandra was restless. The bed was much more comfortable than the old used mattresses on the floor that the cartel had provided her. It was almost too comfortable. Her mind recounted the day's events. Most days leading up to this one were much the same. She would cook, clean, and nurse the sick kids. Every two weeks she would go to Reserva Jaguarundi to perform the inspection, but otherwise, every day was the same. Today was so different and the helicopter ride was the most amazing thing she had ever done. Her mind also tried to imagine what the coming days would be like.

After tossing and turning for almost an hour, exhaustion finally won out and Alejandra drifted off to sleep.

Dim morning light showed through the sheer curtains as Victoria woke from a dream of relaxing at the beach watching Richie surf. The previous night's conversation had focused her mind on her younger days. She felt good but a bit drained from the events of the past couple of weeks. She had traveled back and forth across the globe in high-stress situations and needed a bit of time to decompress.

The first thing she would do today would be to find some towels or a blanket to hang over that window. Victoria liked it pitch black when she slept and if she was ever going to sleep past sunrise she would need to find a way to keep the light out.

Stumbling into the kitchen, Victoria was a bit surprised to see Alejandra already pouring water through the sock to make coffee. It was the traditional way to make coffee in Costa Rica and Victoria believed it was the best way. Alejandra was pouring the water slowly allowing the water to sit in the coffee grounds longer to create a stronger cup. Alejandra smiled at Victoria but did not speak. Her conditioning with the cartel had taught her not to speak until spoken to. With the morning version of Victoria, this was probably best. She could be a real bear in the morning, and you never knew what kind of mood she was in until after she had her coffee.

"Good morning," Victoria grumbled with a half-hearted smile. "How did you sleep?"

Alejandra let the last few drops fall into the mug before handing it to Victoria and placing one for herself under the sock. "Once I fell asleep it was amazing, thank you. I had trouble getting my mind to stop after all of yesterday's excitement."

"I understand," Victoria said as she headed to the porch to take in the sunrise cresting the hills to the east.

After a few minutes, she turned around to see Alejandra standing in the kitchen with her cup of coffee in hand. She seemed unsure of what to do or where she was supposed to be. Victoria waved at her to join her on the porch. Alejandra, still unsure of this new situation, approached cautiously with her cup of coffee.

The women stood in silence for a few minutes taking in the moment and allowing the liquid go juice to take effect. The caffeine stirred the synapsis in Vic's brain and she began to consider the plans for the day.

"I have a meeting with my team this morning," started Victoria. "when that's done, we will go shopping for some clothes and any items you need."

"Can I meet your friends?" asked Alejandra timidly. "I would like to tell them thank you for helping rescue me."

"Well..." Vic knew that the more Alejandra

knew about the team, the more the cartel would torture her if they ever captured her again. "It's too dangerous, both for you and for them right now. But I tell you what, if you want to record a message for them, I will share it in our meeting."

Alejandra nodded her acceptance of the terms. The women sat on the porch and enjoyed the moment. They didn't speak but simply allowed the day to start uninterrupted. Alejandra was surprised and a bit unsure when Victoria took her cup to refill it. It had been many years since anyone had waited on her. Victoria had said nothing but simply grabbed the near-empty mug and headed to the kitchen. She returned with a steaming hot fresh cup and handed it to Alejandra without a word, just a simple smile.

The hillside was coming to life and the birds increased the volume of chirping. The howler monkeys in the distance were making their presence known. The sky was mostly clear with only a few wispy clouds that reflected orange and red light from the sunrise. The fragrant air was thick with moisture from the previous night's rain.

Vic's phone vibrated an alert. It was Ivan with meeting instructions.

"Thanks for not ruining it," Vic said, returning her gaze to the view from the porch.

"Ruining what?" asked Alejandra.

"The moment," replied Victoria. "So many people, and especially us women, like to talk. It is as if the silence is unbearable, and the moment is not enough."

"You're welcome," Alejandra replied.

Since she was not allowed in the meeting and it wasn't safe for her to go out alone, Vic set Alejandra up in front of the television. It would occupy her time while Vic was in the meeting and give her a chance to see what the modern world is like and it would occupy her time until the meeting was finished.

Vic sat on her bed, leaned back against the wall, and opened her laptop. A few clicks later and she was watching Ivan take a drink from his Deadpool mug. She brushed her hair behind her right ear and said, "Good morning, Ivan. We have a lot to discuss."

CHAPTER 21
DEBRIEFINGS AND DISCOVERIES

"Good to see you, Vic," Ivan greeted. "The others are logged in and I will connect them now."

The screen flashed and the faces of each team member appeared on the side in a row of boxes. Imri and Gordo's faces looked fairly happy and welcoming, while Camilo, Guayo, and The Skipper had somber expressions. It was to be expected, from one perspective the mission was an incredible success but from another, it required a sacrifice that was tough to swallow.

"Good morning gentlemen," Vic addressed the team. "I want to start by saying I am grateful for everything Chepe did for us and am so sorry we lost him. I know there is nothing I can say to ease the pain, but please know that I understand what you are feeling. We have all served with great men who have fallen at our sides. He loved Camilo and Robby enough to knowingly take the risk regardless of the cost. I know that I am personally in his debt because his suppressive fire is what allowed us to slip away."

"How many more?" Camilo asked gruffly. "How many more have to die for your vendetta?"

"Give her a break, Camilo," The Skipper stepped in to defend Vic. "When Robby was taken you would have done anything to get him back. And if he would have been killed, you would chase his killers to the ends of the earth to take their lives. You of all people should understand."

Guayo spoke up, "If asked, Chepe would do it again."

Nobody spoke for 15 seconds. Vic broke the silence, "Again, I'm sorry we lost Chepe. At the present time, we are all in danger of retaliation from the cartel. We need to be focused. They do not like losing and based on the ratio of our team to theirs, we definitely won that battle. We need to protect ourselves because they will come after us.

Since so much happened and we were two separate teams I think we need to know what happened with each team and where that leaves us now. I'll start with my report on what happened with my team. Gordo feel free to jump in with any important details I may be missing..."

As Vic recounted her team's experience, Gordo made sure to jump in and let everyone know that she took two rounds to the vest while covering Robby. The look on Camilo's face softened slightly hearing that Vic had shielded her cousin and taken the hit herself. Vic talked about their firefight near the river and how Gordo had covered their take-off to the point of spie rigging for the escape.

"I gotta tell you," Gordo inserted with a grin, "that was one of the most beautiful flights I've ever taken. The jungle is amazing at sunset!"

"I would like to hear what happened to the rest of you," Vic said more as a directive than a question.

"Yeah, Vic," The Skipper stepped in, "I know it may have seemed I jumped the gun a bit with the sea-whiz."

"Yeah, what the fuck was that?" asked Vic. "I don't recall, "light up the beach with 75 rounds per second of 20mm lead" being part of the plan. I didn't even know that was an option."

The Skipper smirked, "Well, I don't always show and tell." He paused for a moment and then continued his report. "There were gunboats approaching fast and the boys were going to be sitting ducks. Imri was not going to be able to take them out fast enough. I had to act, and I thought an overwhelming show of force might help create chaos and an opportunity for you to slip away."

"It wasn't my plan," Vic said, "but it sounds like your call may have been the game changer we needed to get the upper hand.

The Skipper, Camilo, and Imri took turns telling the actions of the other team. Guayo did not add anything but gave confirming nods at different points in the report. The mood of the meeting took a positive swing as the men took turns discussing the battle and their confirmed kills. As the story unfolded, they saw more clearly how fortunate they were that Chepe was the only casualty.

When it came to the part where Chepe was shot, the mood swung back to a somber tone.

"It was bad luck really," Camilo said. "If he wouldn't have spun, the round would have been taken by the vest. Those lucky sons of bitches landed one in the side between the plates."

"He didn't suffer long," Guayo added, trying to take comfort in the circumstance of Chepe's death. "He died fighting for people he loved. He died a hero and that is exactly what he wanted. Chepe never wanted to grow old and wither away in a chair on a porch somewhere or in a hospital."

"You're right," Camilo conceded. "He went out fighting like he would have wanted."

After another short moment of silence, The Skipper continued the report. "As the boys were dealing with Chepe, we had another issue arise with the coast guard..." The Skipper told the others about the escape in the night through the storm. When it got to the part of the helicopter picking up the men, Camilo took over and continued updating to when they were dropped off at Robby's resort.

"And that's when we connected with Robby and Gordo," Camilo said. "But you weren't there. All Gordo told us is that you went somewhere to keep a promise to someone. Where are you?"

"Yeah," Vic sat up and prepared to deliver the report of Alejandra and the server room, "I've got a bit more to share. Imri, do you remember the woman on the container ship that helped us with the trafficked kids?"

"Sure," Imri responded.

"Do you remember me asking Gregario about her?" She continued.

"Yes," the wheels began to turn in his mind as he recalled the interrogation, and he was beginning to see the problem. "You went after her, didn't you?"

"As the drugs wore off, Gregario was going to remember me asking about her. He knew there was a connection, and I am certain he would have tortured her to find out anything he could about me. There's even a chance he would have put it together that she helped us with the kids somehow. I couldn't take the risk of her being hurt because of me."

The men listened as Vic explained her reasoning for going in alone. She described the farmhouse and how she and Alejandra avoided being caught by the guards in the house. Vic talked about the long tunnel and the server room that it led to.

"What's with all the computers?" asked Gordo.

"Priya and I can shed a little light on that once Vic is done with her debriefing," said Ivan.

"Okay," said Vic quizzically. "Well, Alejandra and I slipped out when one of the guards returned with one of the drugged dogs. I think Gregario must have placed a call at that time because the guards began to scramble and were calling out for Alejandra. With Ivan's help, we made our way to a shack in the woods, and I procured wheels to the LZ"

Vic wrapped up the rest of the journey to the safe house. She did not talk about the night of bonding she had with Alejandra. They did not need to know what the women had shared about themselves and their lives. They would not have been interested in or understood the significance of the traditional meal. The calm beautiful moment of coffee, sunrise, and silence was not part of the report either.

With the men caught up to the present, Vic turned their attention to Ivan. "So, what were you saying you and Priya learned about that server room?"

Ivan finished his swig of coffee and lowered his Deadpool mug. "First, I thought it was interesting that we did not know it was there. Usually, we are able to know where large processing centers are because governments and other interested parties monitor the amount of power pulled from the grid. Whoever built this system knew what they were doing. They are not connected to the power grid. They pull their power directly from the wind farm that is adjacent to the property. Part of the farm is connected to the grid, so it appears everything is legit. But with a little digging, I was able to determine that the majority of the turbines are supplying power solely to the server room."

Priya interjected, "I crosschecked passport records with people who are known to have the skills to build a room like this, both technologically and structurally. There were three people who have what it takes to create and set up that space and were in Costa Rica in the past three years. I did more digging and found out that Jamie Alvarado graduated with dual master's degrees in computer science and engineering from Georgia Tech. What's more, he had a cousin who attended with him his first two years. That cousin's name was Alvin Leonardo Alvarado..."

"Let me guess," Vic interrupted, "his cousin is Leo."

"You guessed it," Priya replied.

"I'm pretty sure that is who I saw at the terminal. The reflection wasn't perfectly clear, but I thought he looked a lot like Leo." Vic said.

"Georgia Tech," Gordo interjected, "that's a great school." Gordo always had an appreciation for higher education. He immediately thought of a rower on the Georgia Tech team who sat seat four. That guy was a powerhouse that pushed his team to be better than they should have been.

"So, what's with the computers?" Camilo was less interested in Leo and his family than in why there was an underground computer room in the hills.

"Well," said Ivan, "that's a great question."

Priya inserted herself, "So far, we have decoded two purposes the server array; data collection, and crypto mining."

"Crypto mining?" repeated Camilo. "You mean cryptocurrency like Bitcoin?"

"I mean exactly like Bitcoin. The owner of those servers is mining BTC along with a few other coins." Priya said proudly. "I was able to break into one of the servers and tracked the hash sent to a set of verification servers. Basically, yes, I assume it is one of these cartels that is mining Bitcoin."

"In addition to the mining," Ivan took over, "to say that the amount of personal data collection in that room was impressive would be a gross under-statement. I have been trying to access more of the system, but the layers of security are beyond anything I have seen before. I was able to access files on a few people of interest and they knew details that I have no idea how they acquired."

"I think it is safe to say that that room is controlled by the CAC," Vic said. "Technology isn't really the Gulf Cartel's mode of operation."

"What does that have to do with us," asked Camilo. "How does that change Vic's mission to take out Gregario?"

"Well," Ivan began to explain, "we have had breaches to our system. This technology may have something to do with that."

"Leo knew who I was," Vic stepped in. "We have no idea how he learned my identity and how much he knows about me, or any of us for that matter. He was able to identify Robby, track him down, and take him."

"He knew how to create a tactical advantage at the beach with the gunboats," Imri added. "If it weren't for The Skipper's little surprise of the Phalanx, that operation would have gone much differently."

"Ivan, can you take down their system?" Vic

asked. "I don't want to right now, but do you have the capability?"

"No," Ivan replied. "I will see if I can plant a virus or find a way to execute a kill command on the system but so far, I am struggling just to access the data."

"See what you can come up with," Vic instructed. "I am quite certain we will need to be able to take out their system if we ever plan to be safe."

"So, what's next?" asked Imri.

"We need to lay low and let the dust settle for a minute," said Vic.

"Can we afford to sit still?" asked Gordo. "The cartels lost men on the beach, and you just stole one of their assets in Alejandra. I know she may be a small piece in their operation, but they need someone to manage their inventory and feed the men."

"Was she able to give any intel on the cartel?" Camilo asked.

"Not yet," answered Vic. "She didn't have access to any of the major players. Chances are it will be the details that she doesn't know are important that will be most useful to us. I will continue to probe but I think actionable intel will be slow..."

As Vic was finishing her sentence the connection dropped and the screen went black. Vic slapped her laptop screen and tapped on the keys but nothing.

CHAPTER 22
THE ROUTINE

Vic's phone vibrated on the table with an alert from Ivan. "Connection lost, what happened? Are you good?"

Vic's mind raced with possible causes for the system crash. She wondered if Leo, or more directly his cousin, was able to hack their connection again and somehow take down their network. Had they planted a virus or something? Or was it something less ominous? Maybe the laptop Ivan had procured for her was defective.

Vic pushed back from the desk and traced the power cord from the laptop. The cord was securely connected to the laptop and the plug was in the wall, but it was not fully seated. Apparently, the computer had not charged, and the battery had died. Vic was so focused on the debriefing that she hadn't noticed the low battery icon. She pushed in the plug, waited a few seconds, and powered the system back on.

She sent a response to Ivan, "Battery died, I'll be back in a moment."

While Vic waited for the computer to get a bit of charge, she checked on Alejandra. Peeking out the door, she saw Alejandra leaning in and paying close attention to the television as she slowly took bites of fresh mango. She was watching the news and the report was on self-driving cars.

Vic closed the door and returned to the table to fire up the laptop. Once reconnected she apologized for the disruption. "Sorry everyone, simple power issue. All is good."

"Thank God," said Imri, "I was waiting for that slick son of a bitch Leo to pop up on the screen again."

"You and me both, buddy," said Camilo.

"Thanks for the faith, guys," Ivan said, only slightly kidding. "I assure you they will not be crashing our meetings again."

"Don't get overconfident Ivan," Vic warned. "I think these players are formidable opponents to your tech prowess." Not wanting to damage his ego, she added, "I'm not saying they are better; I'm saying you need to keep your guard up because they are worthy adversaries."

Turning her focus back to the rest of the team she continued. "We all need to be on guard. We can be sure that Gregario will not sit back and lick his wounds. He will retaliate, it's not a question of if, it is when, where, and who."

"Agreed," The Skipper chimed in. "What I know of the man is that he does not take losing gracefully. He is likely to turn this whole thing into a dumpster fire. He has been known to take nuclear measures, wiping out entire villages because one man crossed him."

"The question I have is, how much leverage does he have with the CAC?" Gordo asked. "I'm less concerned with the capabilities of his organization than I am of the CAC."

"That's a great question," Vic said. "We can play the "what if" guessing game all day, but it's best to focus on what we know. For now, let's keep our heads down and watch for threats. Speaking of threats, I need someone to keep an eye on Alejandra's daughter Cynthia. I don't want Gregario snatching her up to use as leverage. She lives near Playa Ostional. Any volunteers?"

Guayo spoke up, "I can handle it. I have family down the road in Nosara that I can visit and who will help keep an eye on her."

"Thanks, Guayo. Priya, please send Guayo her bio and photos." Instructed Vic. "Ivan, I need you to focus on the security of our network and accessing what you can from the server room."

"I'll send the info in three minutes," Priya acknowledged.

"Got it Vic," said Ivan.

"Camilo, take care of Robby," Vic continued. "I know he is shaken up over his recent experience, but he is stronger than you might think. It may not be a bad idea to give him some basics on how to protect himself. I don't want Gregario snatching him up again."

"Skipper, handle your boat repairs. I'll call you if I need your help."

"Whatever you need, Vic," said The Skipper.

"Imri, head home to heal," she continued.

"I think you need all hands on deck," Imri objected. "I can't help from halfway across the globe."

"I need you at your best and that requires you to rest and heal," said Vic.

"Gordo..." Vic started.

"Don't even think about sending me packing," Gordo interrupted. "You need backup whether you like it or not. I'm coming to you. Ivan, send me coordinates."

Not waiting for another objection from Vic, Ivan replied quickly, "Sending them now."

"Wait a minute," Vic balked. "I need to build trust with Alejandra to try to extrapolate intel. I can't do that with you hovering around. If you insist on backing me up, you must do it from afar. You can be overwatch and provide surveillance."

"I accept that," agreed Gordo.

With assignments divied? out, the team gave their final thoughts and signed off. Now it was time for Victoria to spend some time with Alejandra. She needed to teach her how to go unnoticed and blend in with the crowd. The first step was getting her clothes that didn't look like they belonged to a homeless person. It was time for a makeover.

Before they left the safe house, Vic gave Alejandra a crash course on the basics to help keep her safe. She told her to avoid eye contact with the people on the streets but not to just stare at the ground. She needed to be aware of her surroundings and look for potential threats. Vic told

Alejandra to look for cameras and try to avoid them. She showed her when she did need to pass in front of a camera how to position her head, hair, and body to minimize the camera's ability to get a clear shot of her face.

Vic covered contingencies for what to do if they got separated. She programmed her and Ivan's numbers into a burner phone and emphasized to Alejandra to keep it on her at all times. Most importantly, Vic established a location for Alejandra to go to should something happen to Vic.

"Do not wait," Vic instructed. "Do not think, just go. Someone from my team will meet you at the church next to the river. Go inside and wait in the nursery."

"How will I know that they are one of your friends?" Alejandra asked.

"We will use a "safe word"," answered Vic. "Mickey Mouse"

"Mickey Mouse?" questioned Alejandra. "Like the cartoon?"

"Exactly," Vic confirmed.

Vic sent a quick text to Ivan informing him of Alejandra's safe word. She wrapped up the instruction and the women headed to the store. There was not much in the way of shopping in the village of the safe house, so they took a drive to a town nearby.

"I'm driving, so you get to play DJ again," Victoria said with a shrug.

"Okay," Alejandra responded. "I will find something good on the radio."

After snubbing her nose at a few traditional stations and ballads, she stopped at a station that was playing "Flowers" by Miley Cyrus. Victoria immediately began singing along and by the time they hit the chorus a second time, Alejandra had joined in with a mixture of singing and humming. The station apparently played top hits from all genres because the next song had a reggae beat and the women shifted from singing to bobbing their heads and swaying to the beat.

At the store, they were able to find some jean shorts and tank tops along with some tennis shoes and jackets. Victoria wanted Alejandra to feel pretty so she picked out a couple of sundresses and sandals as well. At the register, she grabbed a couple of bottles of nail polish and clippers. They made another stop at the grocery store where they picked up razors, tweezers, and makeup basics. Wearing one of their new outfits, the women proceeded to the last stop, a hairstylist.

Before they entered the shop, Vic had a few instructions for Alejandra. "They are going to want to talk. They will ask you all about yourself, that is part of their job. This is a chance for you to practice making up a story. Do what you can to avoid telling them anything about your past."

Alejandra nodded as she took in the instructions.

"You can be honest about general things like your favorite color, the foods you like, or places in the world you hope to visit someday. But the goal is that they do not really know anything about you. Can you do that?"

"I think so," answered Alejandra. "I'm not very good at lying though."

"Try not to think about it as lying," Vic advised. "Think of it as acting."

"Got it," said Alejandra confidently.

"But before you start your acting practice, you need to decide what hairstyle you want." Victoria was hoping she would change it up a bit. "You can even change the color if you like. Just remember, nothing too flashy that people would remember like bright red or purple."

Alejandra's hair was quite long so she chose to shorten it up a bit. Not too short though, she still wanted to be able to braid it easily to keep it out of her face on hot days. She chose to forgo the color until she was not trying to be discreet. Although it did not completely change her look, the new style was enough to make it a bit more difficult to identify her.

With a fresh hairdo and new outfits, the women enjoyed the ride back to the safe house. More singing, more dancing, and even a bit of conversation. Alejandra told Victoria about a girl at the farmhouse with an amazing voice. The story did not reveal any real intel, but it was a start. It would likely be simple conversations like this that Alejandra would share a small detail of value. The important thing was that Alejandra opened up and shared what she remembered.

Vic knew that it was important to keep their minds and bodies active. Sitting around the safe house and watching time pass can become unbearable without a purpose. They could not afford to get weaker, Vic wanted to make sure they used the time to gain strength instead. It was her goal to restore Alejandra's self-image and confidence that years with the cartel had drained from her. She hoped she could help her develop some skills to protect herself as well. In the days that followed, the women established a routine.

Their days began with coffee and breakfast on the porch in silence as they watched the sunrise. The women would let breakfast settle as they cleaned up breakfast and took care of housekeeping. Before the heat of the day got too intense, Vic would lead exercises and Alejandra would do her best to keep up. Then, they would shower and get cleaned up, and spend some time reading or watching television. This helped Alejandra get caught up with current events. Vic would get brief updates from Ivan regarding the whereabouts of Gregario, any news of the cartels' searches for them, updates on the other team members, and progress accessing the servers.

In the evening Vic would instruct Alejandra on self-defense tactics, as well as weapons familiar-ization and safety. They would practice drawing and dryfiring to increase comfort and speed. After a break to watch the sunset, the women would venture out under the cover of night to spend some time outside the safe house. Vic showed Alejandra how to use the shadows to move through the darkness unseen. Usually, they would conclude the nighttime excursions with a run back to the safe house.

They would wrap up the day by spending some time talking on the couch and enjoying a sweet treat or a nightcap. Victoria would try to update Alejandra on the major global events of the past several years while she was captured. The cartel had kept her isolated from civilization and the culture had changed quite a bit since she was an active member of it. Vic would also gently probe Alejandra for stories and information on the cartel. Every so often Alejandra would divulge the identity of a cartel member or recall stories of their exploits she had overheard. The process was slow, but Vic was starting to collect pieces of the puzzle that were giving insight into the cartel's dealings and the primary players involved.

Ivan had arranged housing for Gordo north of the safehouse with line-of-site to the front of the safe house. While the women were out on a run, Gordo had installed remote cameras with motion detectors in the trees to monitor the back of the house. If anyone tried to approach the house, he should see them coming.

It was the common belief that it wasn't a matter of IF someone would come after the women, but rather when. All they could do is prepare for an attack and hope they would have moved on before anyone discovered the location of their safe house. For now, they were relatively safe, but how long it would last was anyone's guess.

CHAPTER 23
THE EVENING RUN

"Vic, I found Gregario," Priya's voice sounded cheerful through the phone. "I intercepted chatter from his men calling for his doctor to come and check him out. He is holed up in one of his mansions outside of Matamoros, Tamaulipas, Mexico."

"That makes sense," Vic replied. "That is close to the cartel headquarters so he will have plenty of backup at his disposal should anyone attack him again. Did they say what was wrong with him?"

"All I caught was something about his stomach and not sleeping," answered Priya.

"He probably has an ulcer from worrying about us," said Vic smugly. "Let's hope whatever it is doesn't kill him before I get a chance to. Good work Priya, stay on it and let me know if anything changes. Also, monitor for any talk regarding our people."

"On it," Priya acknowledged. "If I hear anything new, I'll let you know right away."

Vic rejoined Alejandra on the couch where she was watching a report about an LGBTQ+ march in San Jose. Alejandra had a confused look on her face. Some of the kids that she cared for at the farmhouse were in this group, but she thought they were made that way by the cartel. Growing up she knew a few gays but not anyone who was transgender, nonbinary, etc. When she was taken there were only boys and girls, not all these other variations. It seemed very strange and a bit confusing to her especially when they talked about the various pronouns. The world had changed.

It had been 13 days since they arrived at the safe house. It struck Victoria how healthy Alejandra was looking. The good quality food and exercise were transforming her into a beautiful woman on the outside. Thanks to Victoria's encouragement and the positive environment her attitude and character were blossoming as well. Overall, she was healing from captivity quite well and she looked good.

Pointing at the television, Victoria asked, "So, what's your type?"

"My type?" Alejandra was taken off guard by the question. "I don't know, it has been so long since I thought of anything romantic for myself. I can tell you I am much more traditional than those people on tv."

"Me too," agreed Victoria. "I can appreciate a beautiful woman, but I don't feel attracted to them like I am to a strong fit man with a nice smile and good manners. I may not understand a lot of the extreme individuals, but I try to respect them as human beings."

"I think for me I would just like a thoughtful man who can make me laugh," answered Alejandra. "I don't care as much if they are super fit or very handsome, but I do want them to be healthy. I guess at this point in my life, I simply want someone who is kind to me."

Victoria concurred, "Don't we all."

Vic's phone buzzed on the table, and she got up to check the message. It was from Imri, "Leg's better." Not only was she glad to hear he was better, but it got her mind considering their next move. Her conviction for Gregario's end at the cause of her hands was still the ultimate goal. Imri would be another much-needed gun. But how were they going to keep Alejandra, Cynthia, and Robby safe?

Guayo had reported that men were watching Cynthia a week ago. Leo obviously knows where Robby's resort is and probably where he lives too. Why hadn't Gregario's men moved on either of them? What was he waiting for? Perhaps it wasn't his decision. Perhaps Leo had seen the bigger threat in Vic and her team, and he was just trying to lay a trap. Vic knew that they could only hide for so long. She had to figure out how to stay ahead of the cartels.

Later that evening, Gordo watched as the women departed the house to begin their daily run. He used a lightweight drone with infrared optics that Ivan had sent to track them on their course and assess threats. Aside from a few drug users that hung out down the road, there was rarely anyone on their path. His attention to the drone was interrupted by a chirp from the motion detectors at the back of the house. Someone had tripped the sensors and activated the cameras.

Gordo set the autopilot on the drone and turned his focus to the monitors. Two men in tactical gear were climbing over the hedge and onto the back porch with rifles drawn.

"Hostiles at the house," was Gordo's message notification on Vic's watch.

"Listen," Vic kept the pace heading away from the house as she began her instructions. "There is trouble back at the house."

Alejandra's face changed from excited about the run to great concern. "¿Qué hacemos?"

"My team is working on it as we speak." Vic tried to temper Alejandra's concern. "We have to keep our heads clear. Control your emotions, do not let them control you."

Alejandra nodded and collected herself. Vic wasn't telling her not to be afraid, she was telling her to acknowledge it and then address it. "Run if you must, but don't give up without a fight," was Vic's advice during the self-defense training. "They are counting on you not fighting back," Alejandra remembered Vic repeating over and over. She would be alert, assess her situation, and react accordingly.

"I need you to do exactly what I say when I say it," Vic commanded. "You are scared, good. It's there to remind you to protect yourself and don't let your guard down."

She led a loop back to the church. Gordo had already left his perch to head for the church. "Do you remember what I told you to do if we were separated?" Vic asked

"Claro" answered Alejandra.

"Good, my backup Gordo will be waiting for us there." Vic gave Alejandra a heads-up that there would be someone from her team at the church just in case she was unable to make the introduction.

"Gordo?" Alejandra asked.

"Sí," Vic confirmed.

Vic took a small path that ran along the property of a big white concrete and stucco house. It was old, abandoned, and overgrown giving off a haunted vibe. The canopy of trees overhead gave the feeling of descending through a tunnel as the trail turned downhill. The moon's light was almost completely obscured by the clouds and the canopy. Only faint wisps of light broke through gaps in the leaves.

The thick humid air filled the women's lungs with oxygen that fed their brains. Running was providing an outlet for the growing nervous tension. Their muscles were warmed up and ready to perform. They ran at a quick pace, closing the distance to the church.

Vic heard a skid of dirt and a scream as Alejandra was clotheslined off her feet. Vic slid to a stop and turned to see her hit the ground with a solid thud. Alejandra's head slammed against the dirt, and she became dizzy trying to decipher what had just happened.

"Leo!" it was more of an uncontrollable expression than a statement. Vic's mind calculated its attack.

Six meters away, he was turned with his right side facing, no drawn weapons. Alejandra was in danger, Vic lunged, closing her distance, and prepared to strike. Leo stood steady and did not flinch at Vic's advance. He was not intimidated by her in the least and didn't seem to respect her skill.

She launched a Superman punch and Leo grabbed her incoming fist and pulled hard, diverting it and throwing Vic tumbling to the ground. She followed the momentum and continued her roll to a fighting stance opposite of where she started. She was between him and Alejandra.

"Run!" Vic commanded, not even questioning if Alejandra was in any condition to flee. Alejandra shook her head and regained her strength. She got to her feet just as Vic began a flurry of fists and heels at Leo to create an opening. Alejandra slipped past the scuffle, gaining speed with every step. Vic did everything she could to keep Leo focused on her and not Alejandra. He deflected her attacks with master technique. Vic lunged and was able to grab a leg pulling him to the ground. She jumped on top and swung at his face with all she had as he blocked her assault with his arms.

Leo punched his arm to Vic's left side and used his strength to throw her off. They got to their feet and began exchanging and deflecting blows. Vic connected with a spinning back fist and stomach kick combo sending Leo falling backward, only to roll to his feet. He returned the volley with a spinning back kick right jab combo that dropped Vic to the ground. She reached behind her and pulled her Sig from her elastic holster. As she swung the barrel in Leo's direction, he kicked it out of her hand and sent it deep into the brush. Leo attempted to draw his weapon, but Vic grabbed his wrist with her left hand and broke it free with her right. The melee continued.

Vic spun to her feet and tackled Leo, throwing him to the ground where she began another assault of fists, landing a few. Between blows, a light shined in Vic's eyes disturbing her night vision and blinding her. Seeing lights approaching, Vic tried to get up and flee, but Leo grabbed her ankle and tripped her. She stumbled as she gained her feet. She took five steps down the path and was met with a muzzle. She turned and saw another hostile approaching from the north path beyond Leo. Turning back, she quickly disarmed her attacker, jumped up and grabbed the low-hanging limb above her, and kicked him square in the chest. Dropping to the ground she raced down the path away from the men.

The other gunman fired his weapon, and she heard Leo yell, "I want her alive. I'll get her. Follow me." Vic was praying the men had been given orders to only shoot her as a last resort. She used her adrenaline and conditioning to sprint away from the men as fast as she could. Although she was terribly slow as a child, over the years she had worked on her stride and developed into quite the runner.

Seeing a split in the path, Vic took the trail to the right to avoid leading the men to the church. Her first priority was Alejandra's safety. Trees lined the footpath, and the trail was rougher than the main path. Looking through the trees over her shoulder she could see two lights from the gunmen back around the bend. Her night vision was not optimal after the gunman had shined it on her, so she was not able to see Leo in the darkness. She didn't realize that although the gunmen were falling behind, Leo was keeping pace. She had scouted this path and realized that it was leading to a dead end.

She had to keep the men from finding Alejandra before Gordo could get her to safety. She reached the path's terminal, a wide lookout circle with a 270º view of the valley and a picnic table in the center. There were matching wooden benches on opposite sides of the table facing out to their side of the landscape. Just past the circle was a cliff of volcanic rock. She did not have time to scale down the wall without her capture or slipping and falling to her death. There was no way out, she had to try to overtake them and escape back down the path.

She stood atop the picnic table and established her fighting stance. Her hope was that the elevated position would give her an advantage. It would be three-on-one with Leo as the strongest opponent. Her attacks on the other two would need to incapacitate them so that she could deal with Leo alone.

As her mind completed processing her surroundings and weighing her options, she spotted Leo emerging from the darkness of the trail. He had blood oozing from his lip and a smug on his face. He seemed to really enjoy his line of work and loved the sport of Vic's fight.

CHAPTER 24
"2IR"

Entering the circle, Leo stopped running and slowly walked toward Vic. He straightened his belt, brushed some dirt from his shoulder, and squared away his shirt. His eyes were locked on Vic's as he brushed his hair back with his left hand. The pair sized each other up while the gunmen finally reached the clearing. They shined their lights on Vic, and one guarded the path while the other slowly circled toward the bench to her left; both with weapons sited on Vic.

"Quite the little conejo," Leo said. "You're pretty fast Victoria. These guys couldn't keep up." His thumbs pointed at the men behind him.

"How did you find me, Leo?" Vic asked.

"Let's just say, we see all, hear all, and know all," he replied.

He had an arrogance about him that was irritatingly likable. If Vic thought about it, she would have to admit she kind of enjoyed the volleys they had exchanged.

"You'd like me to think it was your superior technical prowess." Vic quipped back. "But actually, it was probably just some poor town person who saw me and was willing to tell you about it for a little money. You know, the old-fashioned way of finding a person." She knew Leo's pride would not accept him being identified as being anything but cutting edge.

"Well, regardless, here we are," he said, taking another step closer. "shall we stroll back down the path and collect Alejandra?"

"Leave her out of this," Vic commanded. "She is not his property and never was."

"That is not my concern," Leo said glibly. "My associate requests both of your presence and I simply oblige. It's not personal, it's just business."

"Well, it's personal to me," Vic retorted.

"So, you're going to resist," Leo asked, smile widening. "I was hoping you would."

He lunged for her legs, and she kicked for the

side of his head. He blocked the kick but was not able to grab her. She jumped over him and went for the guard that was circling. Using her momentum, she slid forward and swept his legs. As his back hit the ground, she dropped her leg on his stomach knocking the wind from his lungs. Getting back to her feet, she grabbed his gun and swung it in Leo's direction.

She was not quick enough, and he kicked it from her grasp before she could get it raised. The mele continued with Leo and Vic exchanging attacks and counters. Occasionally, they would land a blow or two. They were fairly evenly matched on skill, but Leo's size and reach gave him an advantage. Before long, Vic missed a kick leaving her open for Leo to grab her and pin her down. It was enough for the other guards to collapse on her. They bound her and escorted her out of the lookout and back down the path toward the safe house.

Vic's attack was enough for Alejandra to get away. Adrenaline fueled Alejandra's muscles, and she did not get winded. Her time with Vic had put her in the best shape of her life. She was afraid but felt more equipped to handle it than ever before. She truly was a new woman. And what this woman is capable of is anyone's guess. It only took her six and a half minutes to reach the church.

Inside, the altar candles illuminated a hallway opening to the left of them with a sign for the nursery. Alejandra's heart raced from the run as well as fear. Entering the dark hallway, she ran her hands along the wall to guide her to a doorway. There was no one in sight and she could not hear anyone there. She opened the door and with the light from the window, she was able to make out a crib and a rocking chair. Alejandra slid inside and closed the door behind her. She pulled a crucifix from the wall and held it like a sword as she waited for someone to find her.

Gordo had arrived a few minutes before Alejandra arrived, but he did not go inside. He found a position on the edge of the property where he could watch and see if she was being tailed. He watched Alejandra enter the church and waited a minute to ensure it was clear before he went in to retrieve her.

Alejandra could hear footsteps approaching down the hall. She grasped the crucifix tightly and prepared to attack. She did not know who was coming but assumed it was one of the men who attacked them on the path. Her mind replayed Vic's instructions, "Don't give up without a fight."

Gordo stopped at the door and knocked softly. "I'm Mickey Mouse and I'm here to take you to Disneyland," he whispered through the door. He turned the knob and slowly opened the door to see Alejandra wielding the crucifix in his direction. His gear did not look much different from the men on the path, so she was a bit unsure at first.

"My name is Gordo," he said, letting his rifle down onto its sling and raising his open hands. "Vic asked me to take you somewhere safe. Alejandra, I need you to come with me." He spoke softly and slowly, and directly, allowing her mind time to process what he was saying.

He had used the safe word they had talked about, and she remembered Vic had said that her friend's name was Gordo. He had found her where Vic had instructed her to go. She had no choice, she had to trust him. She dropped the crucifix and Gordo led her out of the church to a Suzuki Jimny 4x4 parked three blocks away.

Gordo messaged Ivan, "Emergency extract activated. Package collected. Primary MIA."

"Acknowledged. Standing by for update," was Ivan's response. In times like this it was best to keep the information to a minimum due to time management and in case of a breach in communications.

Ivan immediately initiated a mass alert to all team members, except for Vic whose phone was assumed to be compromised.

"21R"

The team knew the message; "2" move to your secondary location, "1" who/if any were compromised, (Vic was number 1, Ivan 2, Camilo 3, etc.), and "R" Reply directly to the sender with your keyword to ensure you're not compromised.

"Terresa" was the first response to Ivan's number from Guayo's phone.

Second was Gordo with "Jacob".

"Maria" Imri's phone was next to respond a moment later.

The Skipper's message read, "Abraham."

"Thomas" Priya's number reported a minute later.

There was a delay of three minutes before Camilo's phone replied, "Joseph".

It was a good effort from whoever sent Camilo's message. The keyword was the team member's location when they attended their first team meeting. The correct response for Camilo would have been, "José", for San José.

Guayo's first location was Playa Santa Teresa in Costa Rica, "Teresa". Jacob's Coffee House on 8th St. in Washington DC was Gordo's, hence "Jacob". Imri first joined at Santa Maria Cathedral in Florence, Italy, "Maria". The Skipper's first meeting was off the coast of Abraham's Bay, The Bahamas, "Abraham." And Priya's was Saint Thomas, U.S. Virgin Islands, "Thomas". All locations checked out except Camilo's.

Ivan sent a video request to Priya. Moments later the two were looking at each other through their webcams. "We need to locate Vic and Camilo and get the others to safety." Ivan started. "I'll focus on locating Vic and Camilo, you work logistics with the others."

"What about Robby?" Priya asked.

"Yes," Ivan said, acknowledging his oversight. His first priority was always the team. "I'll try to identify his location through surveillance, I need you to see what chatter you can intercept about him."

"Not a problem," affirmed Priya. "I'm still tracking Gregario as well. Do you need any help with the servers?"

"Actually," Ivan was grateful for the offer, he respected her skill, "I'm getting a bit of tunnel vision with this one and could use a fresh perspective. But only the first priority is team integrity."

"Sure, but what if the information on those servers would answer all the questions that we need answers for?"

"Good point," Ivan acknowledged, "just make sure you balance priorities.'

"Don't worry, I won't get code locked and lose an entire day. Been there, done that. I'll keep you updated on the team, and I'll let you know if I make any progress on the servers."

As they signed off, Ivan thought about how happy he was that Vic had allowed him to bring her onto the team. Ivan would not have been able to juggle the operational logistic needs of the team and break into the servers on his own. As the team grew so did the number of moving parts. He was thankful to have Priya's contributions.

At the safe house, Vic sat in a kitchen chair with her hands zip-tied behind her back. Leo messaged on his phone while the men ransacked the house looking for Alejandra or a clue about where she went. They collected Vic's laptop and phone. The men completed their search and returned to the kitchen. Leo removed Vic's smartwatch and put it on top of the other electronics. Vic ran scenarios in her head, the best of which involved the butcher block on the counter behind Leo. The risk was too high, she needed to wait for a better opportunity to attack and escape.

"Let's go," said Leo, putting his phone in his pocket.

He grabbed the pile of electronics and headed for the door. The other men grabbed Vic and escorted her outside to a black Prado parked around the corner. They put a hood over her head and pushed her into the backseat. The two men sat on either side of Vic as Leo drove off. Vic traced Leo's turns with the map in her mind. She was doing well until he stopped at a property that she had no reference to.

Vic heard helicopter blades as the truck turned and began to slow to a stop. Vic's opportunities for attack were dwindling. They exited the truck and Vic stomped on the foot of the guard to her right. She blindly threw her head back to connect with his jaw as he was bending over to look at his foot. The blow threw his head back and Leo steadied him with his hand to the guard's back. The other guard struck Vic in the skull with the but of his pistol.

Leo gave her an injection in the neck and the effects slammed Vic's nervous system as she went limp. The men regained control and loaded Vic into the helicopter. She lost consciousness as the helicopter began to lift off. That's the last thing she remembered.

"Priya, I'm tracking a plane heading straight toward Gregario in Matamoros, Tamaulipas that came from Costa Rica" Ivan reported. "Vic's devices went dark one at a time on the way to the airport. I think Leo was disabling each tracker. Her phone was the last to drop off. With the rate of travel, it was clear that she was airborne. It is as if Leo wanted to leave breadcrumbs."

"Got it," Priya replied. "I heard chatter from the cartel of a private party that Gregario is throwing. They said there were two VIP's and one royalty. Do you think that could be Vic, Camilo, and Robby?"

"That would make sense." Ivan agreed.

"I'll get Imri headed in that direction and give him an update," Priya asserted.

"He's going to need backup," Ivan cautioned.

"I'll work out the logistics for one of the others to join him," Priya said.

"Have them set up at our safe house in Brownsville, Texas just across the border," directed Ivan. "Vic set up this house to be able to keep tabs on Gregario about five years ago. It's fully stocked, and tunnels under the house lead across to Matamoros."

"Understood." She said as they closed the connection. Priya was focused and prepared to work out the logistics of assembling the team members.

First, Priya submitted a new flight plan to the USA for Imri. He would arrive in 9 hours. She called to inform him of the new arrangements and gave him the latest status update.

"We assume that Vic is on that flight to Mexico. Even if not, it's our best guess of where they would take her at this point. As soon as we get confirmation, I'll pass it along."

"Copy," acknowledged Imri.

"I will work the logistics for someone to join you. It may take a little time though. In the mean-time, get to the safe house, and gather whatever intel you can. Familiarize yourself with the tunnels, you may need to lead a team through them."

"I will," answered Imri, signing off.

Next, Priya set up a web meeting with Gordo, Guayo, and The Skipper.

CHAPTER 25
GET OUT OF THE COUNTRY

G uayo was the last to log in. Priya used her pointer finger to push her glasses up the bridge of her nose, indicating the connection was secure. Guayo coughed, confirming his end was safe as well.

"It's good to see you all." Priya started. "Ivan is engrossed in hacking the CAC servers and may be on the brink of success, so I'll brief you on the latest intel and then we can talk about the next steps."

The men sat back and took in the information as Priya led her first team meeting. Priya presented a map of North and Central America. She reported how Vic's devices had left a trail to the airport.

Zooming in on the border of Mexico and the USA, she told them about the flight to Matamoros, Mexico, and the chatter of a "private party". Gordo nodded his agreement with her and Ivan's assumption that the party was actually Camilo, Robby, and Vic. She told them about the safe house in Brownsville, USA with tunnels into Matamoros.

"Imri is en route and will await backup at the safe house," Priya concluded the briefing. "Now as to the next steps..."

"We need to get Alejandra out of the country," Gordo spoke up. "Gregario has men scouring the country asking about her. She's not safe here."

"Same for Cynthia," Guayo joined.

"Agreed," Priya began her proposal. "Skipper, do you think you could find a safe place for Cynthia and Alejandra?"

"If you can get them here without the cartel knowing where they went," The Skipper said, "I'll make sure nothing happens to them."

"I'll work with Ivan on transportation logistics to avoid being tracked," Priya confirmed. "Guayo and Gordo, take your assets and head toward the airport in Liberia. We will start with a little shell game at the airport. If you're being followed, we will try to shake the tail there first."

"We're ready to move out immediately," Gordo acknowledged. Guayo nodded, indicating he was ready as well.

"Once you connect at the airport, Gordo, you will catch a flight to meet up with Imri in Texas." Priya continued, "Guayo, you continue to escort Alejandra and Cynthia the rest of the way to The Skipper in Oregon."

"I'll make preparations for their arrival." The Skipper chimed in. "Don't worry, I have the perfect place for them."

"How is Guayo going to convince Cynthia to leave with him?" Gordo asked. "She has no idea who he is, or even that she is in danger. And remember, she hasn't seen her mother in a decade. How do you suppose that reunion will go?"

"Good point," said Priya. "As far as them reuniting, I think it would be best if they didn't see each other until they are en route. The flights will be long, so they will have a lot of time to talk and catch up in transit." The others in the meeting nodded in agreement.

"What if you told her she won a vacation," Priya suggested the first thing that came to mind.

"That is not something that normally happens around here," Guayo said. "And if I tell her she has to leave right away and not pack or anything, I am sure she would get suspicious and refuse to come."

"Okay," Priya saw the errors with that idea. "Anyone else have any suggestions?"

"We don't have time for Guayo to develop trust with her," said Gordo. "Even if he said that he was taking her to her mother, I am not sure she would be convinced to get on a plane with a stranger who is not a member of the police or something. Even if he was law enforcement, I'm not sure she would do it."

"He's going to have to kidnap her," The Skipper interjected. "We don't have time for any other options, and we cannot afford for her to refuse. She may not understand that we are doing it for her own good, but we don't have time to make her understand."

"He's right," agreed Guayo. "I don't have time to convince her to come willingly. I am going to have to force her."

"I think it might be best to drug her," said Gordo. "Perhaps waking up to her mother will help ease the shock of being taken. If you can keep her sedated until she is at 37,000 feet, Alejandra should be able to talk her through what is happening to her. After all, it is because of her relation to Alejandra that she is in danger in the first place."

"That sounds like our best option," agreed Guayo. "I'll head to the farmacia to get supplies and get on the road."

"I hate the idea of drugging and kidnapping an innocent woman, but I guess that it's better than the alternatives," Priya said reluctantly. "Call when you are getting close to the airport, and I will give you the rest of the logistics." The team signed off and Priya got to work on travel arrangements.

Cynthia was working at the Mini Super when Guayo went to collect her. They were closing up for the night and she waved goodbye to her last customer as she locked up and headed toward the dumpster with a stack of cardboard. The road was empty except for a small group of men standing around outside the bar at the far end of town. It often got muggy in the bar so it was common for people to step outside with their drinks to get some fresh air.

Guayo quickly snuck around the opposite side of the shop and hid in the shadows. Softly singing a tune to herself, Cynthia dropped the load into the dumpster and turned to walk back to the front of the store. Guayo silently stepped out from the shadows behind her and quickly administered the injection. She felt a pinch as if she had just been stung and passed out. Guayo caught her fall, scooped her up, and carried her limp body in his arms to the truck. Nobody witnessed the abduction, and they were on their way to the airport in less than twenty minutes from the time of the call.

About halfway to the airport, Gordo thought he spotted a tail. He sped up until the headlights disappeared from his rearview mirror. Alejandra braced as he whipped the truck down a sideroad, pulled off toward the bushes, and killed the lights. A few minutes later an SUV passed and continued on its way. To be safe, Gordo used an alternative route to the airport that put him behind schedule.

As they drove the rest of the way to the airport, Gordo worried about how Alejandra would handle being turned over to a guy that had drugged and kidnapped her daughter. He hoped she would feel a bit more at ease when she realized that Guayo was a Tico like her and that he had family who lived near Cynthia. Guayo was a nice guy, but his quiet demeanor could come across as a bit cold and intimidating. He also needed to prepare Alejandra, since they were counting on her help to explain to Cynthia what was happening.

Gordo told Alejandra that he needed to go rescue Vic. He told her how Vic's team was worried about Cynthia's safety and that they had decided it was best to take them both far away to protect them. Someplace that the cartel wouldn't find them. Alejandra nodded her understanding as he spoke but did not say anything in return.

"A friend of mine and Vic's will meet us at the airport with your daughter," Gordo prepared her. "She does not know what is happening. We did not have time to explain to her why she was in danger and from whom."

Gordo paused for a moment to let that part sink in and for Alejandra's mind to process the situation. The road curved and he swerved left to avoid a pothole left by the recent rains. The head-lights drifted into the dust-covered bushes on the side before recentering on the road ahead.

"She will be unconscious when you take off,"

he continued. "She will wake up on the plane while you are on your way to The United States."

Alejandra's expression showed concern and that her mind was racing. Before she had a chance to begin to question or object, Gordo continued feeding her instructions and information.

"We need you to help keep her calm and explain what is happening," Gordo gave the instructions slowly and clearly. "Your face is the only one that she may recognize as familiar. We are hoping that she will understand better if you tell her and that she may trust us more because of you."

Alejandra turned her eyes back to the road. She began to think about the situation and what she would say to Cynthia. Her time with Vic had grown and developed a strength in her that made it feel like she could face this challenge. She could help protect her daughter.

They did not talk the rest of the way to the airport. Gordo figured that if Alejandra had questions she would ask. He didn't want her getting too caught up in details and getting more anxious. Being on the run was stressful enough. He wanted to give her a chance to take in all that was happening.

Priya hacked the airport system and arranged for three flights to take off back-to-back. That way if anyone spotted them, it would be difficult to know which flight they had boarded. One flight was a commercial flight to Houston, Texas, then on to Denver, Colorado. The second was a charter jet with a flight plan to São Paulo, Brazil. And the third flight was a cargo plane scheduled to deliver in Los Angeles, California.

It would be nearly impossible to get Cynthia on a passenger plane, unconscious, and without anyone raising concerns. The plan was for Gordo to take the commercial flight to Houston, where Priya had a car waiting for him to drive to Brownsville. Guayo, Cynthia, and Alejandra would board the cargo flight. From LAX they would take a seaplane up the coast and land in Coos Bay where they would connect with The Skipper.

A forklift was loading pallets and crates onto the cargo plane when Gordo and Alejandra arrived. Gordo had taken a service road to the edge of the airfield where he spotted Guayo's vehicle parked in the darkness just beyond the lights that lined the fence. Gordo turned his lights down to the parking lights as he slowly pulled up behind him and parked. He could see the barrel of Guayo's rifle pointed at him.

"Don't worry," Gordo said to Alejandra who was breathing quite rapidly. "He's just making sure it is us and that we are alone."

Gordo checked his surroundings as he slowly stepped from the truck, searching for threats. Once Guayo recognized him he dropped his rifle and opened his door to get out. The men agreed the coast was clear and Gordo motioned for Alejandra to get out of the truck and join him. She took a long deep breath, grabbed the handle, and exited the vehicle cautiously.

She looked at the ground where she was step-ping before raising her head to look at the men in front of her. As soon as she was close, Gordo made the introduction, "Alejandra, this is my friend Guayo. He is a good man; he will protect you and get you to safety."

Guayo's cold expression warmed as Alejandra stepped closer. At first, he could not make out her features in the darkness. The closer she got the more she raised her head, and he could see her clearly. There was something about her that he was captivated by. As she approached, his anxiety rose. His mind quickly reminded him that this was the mother of the young woman he had drugged in his pickup. The excitement of the moment was conflicting him.

"Hola, mucho gusto," Guayo offered the standard greeting. It was really all he could come up with. He didn't know how else to greet someone under these circumstances.

CHAPTER 26
ALTITUDE AND ATTITUDE

Alejandra handled the exchange incredibly graciously. She was scared, but clinging to Vic's teachings on bravery. She trusted Victoria, and if these were her people, she had to trust them as well. Looking past Guayo she saw a figure in the truck.

"It's your daughter," Guayo confirmed. "She's unconscious. I did not hurt her; it was only a little sting."

Alejandra breathed in deeply, let the air out, and stepped past Guayo to approach the passenger door of the truck. When her eyes took in the face, her knees buckled, and she grabbed the mirror for support. She was overcome with emotion. She had not seen her little girl in so long.

Here she was, a beautiful young woman. Alejandra's eyes welled up and she brushed away the tears.

"We need to get you all out of sight and on that plane," instructed Gordo as he scanned the horizon.

Alejandra stepped aside as she watched Guayo pick her child up and carry her. Gordo used cutters from the truck to create a hole in the fence. Once the forklift left and the coast was clear, he led the others to the plane and guarded them as they boarded. With them safely on the plane, Gordo crossed the tarmac to the side door of the terminal. He stashed his tactical gear in a maintenance room and headed to the gate to board his own flight.

Alejandra sat up in her seat with her eyes fixed on Cynthia. Guayo had strapped her in next to Alejandra and leaned her head back against a piece of packing foam he had found behind one of the crates. Alejandra took Cynthia's hand and held it in hers as she watched her sleep.

As the crew closed the doors and prepared for takeoff, Alejandra looked over at Guayo. She noticed he was Latino and addressed him in her native tongue, "Where are we going?"

"The United States," Guayo answered.

"Where in The United States?" it was clear that Alejandra wanted details.

"We are landing in Los Angeles," Guayo replied.

"And then?" She pried.

Guayo waited until the crewman stepped into the cockpit to respond.

"And then we take another plane to a safe house in Oregon," he said.

"How long until she wakes up?" she asked.

"In about six hours," he answered. "Not until we are on the next plane."

The engines grew loud, and the plane began to roll. Alejandra reached over and braced Cynthia's head against the foam as the plane took off. She kept her eyes on her, studying every line and curve. She wanted to burn this beautiful face into her memory forever. Time passed without notice as she focused on her daughter and considered what their relationship would be like.

"What are the chances she will recognize me," Alejandra asked, thinking out loud. "Or even remember me?"

Guayo barely heard her over the sound of the jet turbines. He figured the odds were somewhere around fifty-fifty that Cynthia would know that Alejandra was her mother. Seeing the worry on Alejandra's face made him feel like he needed to offer some comfort. He spoke up over the noise of the plane, "It is nature's way that an offspring knows its mother. And I believe that God created us with a spirit that is connected to our family. A lot has happened in the past decade so it might take a moment for her mind to catch up to her heart and spirit. Not to mention that the last thing she will remember is closing the shop and getting stung. It is going to take her a few minutes to hear what is happening. The first thing you need to do is to let her know that she is safe."

Guayo was a man of few words, and this exchange was out of character. There was something about Alejandra that made him open up. Alejandra looked into his eyes and felt warmth. She had just met him, and yet there was something about him that made her feel calm in all this chaos. She had heard what he said, and it resonated in her heart. She prayed that Cynthia would remember her, and that God would give her the right words to explain everything to her.

As the flight continued, Alejandra would look up to find Guayo staring at her. He would try to look away for a moment, but when she turned back to Cynthia, he would look back at her. It was different than the way men had looked at her for as long as she could remember. Not like a piece of meat or an overbearing guard. His expression looked as though he was watching the sunset. It felt nice.

Aside from some minor turbulence crossing Mexico, the rest of the flight was smooth. Alejandra helped transfer Cynthia to the seaplane and get her strapped in. The exchange only took twelve minutes, and they were airborne again.

"How long is this flight?" Alejandra asked over the buzz of the seaplane engine.

"About two and a half hours," replied Guayo from the row behind her.

Alejandra recalled every memory she had of her daughter before she was taken. The time passed quicker than Alejandra anticipated. A couple hours later Cynthia stirred slightly, indicating it wouldn't be long before she regained consciousness. Alejandra gently held her hand and watched her. She used the last moments to pray for guidance.

"Que..." Cynthia's eyes squinted in the light as she searched for her bearings.

The familiar accent of Alejandra's voice gave Cynthia no indication that she was several countries from home. "You are safe, my girl."

"Who...where," Cynthia's mind fought to emerge from the fog as her eyes searched for references.

She rubbed her eyes and strained to identify the woman sitting next to her.

"I am Alejandra, you are on an airplane..." Cynthia struggled to sit up straight and understand what she was hearing.

"You were in danger, but you are safe now."

"Danger?" Cynthia rubbed her eyes some more and looked around. She shied back a bit when she spotted Guayo behind her.

"How did I get here?" her mind was racing.

"Look at me," Alejandra hoped she would recognize her. If nothing else, perhaps looking Alejandra in the eye would help her focus on what she was saying instead of her mind jumping from question to question. She continued slowly, letting each word and phrase sink in.

"Do I look familiar to you?" Alejandra asked.

Cynthia searched for reference as her mind quieted and focused on the question at hand.

"You are... You look... Mama?" Cynthia's

expression changed to a look of shock, question, and heartbreak all at the same time.

"Do you know what happened to me?" Alejandra let Cynthia's mind connect one thing to the next.

"You were taken by the Gulf Cartel," Cynthia said. "Most people said you died many years ago. The moment was too heavy to hold herself together. Her heart got the best of her, and she began to sob. Alejandra tried to be strong for Cynthia and keep her composure, but she let out a few tears as well.

"With some help, I escaped," she continued. "Those men were going to come after you too."

Cynthia looked back at Guayo.

"Not him," Alejandra wasn't sure how she was going to explain that although Guayo had kidnapped her, he was not a threat. She tried to keep the information to the basics and skip over the details. "But the cartel is after both of us now and we are going someplace safe, far away from them."

"Have you ever been to Oregon?" Alejandra was pretty sure she knew the answer, but it might help distract Cynthia from the burning question of how she is finding herself on an airplane.

"What... no," Cynthia was having trouble connecting the next dot.

"I need you to trust me," Alejandra reassured her. "We are going to be okay. I'm not going to let anyone come between us again. And my friends are very good at protecting people."

Cynthia was still struggling to make sense of everything. She felt like this was a dream; like she had put herself into some action movie or something. She looked out the window and saw the ground racing by far below. The landscape was covered in trees, but these trees were not like the ones she was used to. They were pointy cone-shaped pine trees like she had seen in pictures.

"So, who are you?" Cynthia was a fairly outspoken girl and had no trouble asserting herself and she was beginning to think a bit clearer.

"I am a friend of a friend," Guayo answered.

Alejandra spent the last fifteen minutes of the flight telling Cynthia about Victoria and how she not only rescued her and protected her, but also taught her how to be strong and have courage. She told her about the attack on the running path and how Vic had sacrificed herself to allow her to escape.

"Guayo is protecting us while we travel. We are going to stay with one of Victoria's friends in Oregon," again, Alejandra skipped over the part about Cynthia being drugged and abducted. "Do you speak good English?"

Cynthia sounded like she grew up in middle America when she switched languages and said, "I was the best in my class, and nine months out of the year I give directions to tourists that stop at the store. My friends and I quote American movies and sing English music all the time. So yeah, I speak pretty good English."

Turning over her shoulder she asked, "So, you are protecting us, but we're not staying with you?" Cynthia still didn't know what to make of Guayo.

"Correct." Guayo's standard short responses returned.

"Why not?" Cynthia asked.

"Because Vic needs me," Guayo answered.

"And we don't?" she quipped back.

"Well..." Guayo searched for his answer. "The Skipper will make sure you are safe."

"Why doesn't The Skipper go help Vic?" Her tone was thick with attitude as she exaggerated each name. She had obviously moved past being intimidated by him.

"Because he's old." Usually, he was better at controlling his responses, but there was something about this girl that threw him off his game.

"Oh, I see…" Cynthia's attitude reached a new level. "So, we lose the middle-aged, although obviously fit "protector," for the safe old man."

"Mija," Alejandra's natural motherly tone rose, "don't bite the hand that feeds. We need all the help we can get."

Guayo was uncomfortable with the way the conversation was heading, but it was better than her digressing back to how she got here.

"I misspoke," he said, "The Skipper is a fine man, he simply offers a different skill set and has different resources. In this situation, he is better equipped to hide you and keep you safe, while my skills are better suited to getting our friend Vic out of trouble."

"Oh yeah," Cynthia could tell she was getting under his skin and liked to see just how far she could push things, "and what skills are those? You look pretty small for a tough guy."

Fortunately for Guayo, the pilot interrupted with his announcement that they were beginning their descent and would be landing in just a few minutes. Turning her focus to the window,

Cynthia did not see a runway in sight. They were dropping closer and closer to the water and her mind found something new to be concerned about.

"Landing where?" Cynthia's pitch raised along with her anxiety.

Enjoying the shift of attention, Guayo gave another brief answer, "On the water."

"Don't worry mija, it's a seaplane," reassured Alejandra. "It floats on the water."

There was a slight jerk as the plane met with the resistance of the water. The pilot pulled up to the dock where a couple of The Skipper's men quickly tied it off. The pilot cut the engine and Guayo got up to open the door. Checking the surroundings for threats, he stepped out onto the pontoon.

"Welcome my new friends, I'm The Skipper." He came across more like a tour guide than a man assigned to protect them. Guayo was almost surprised he didn't come with umbrella drinks in hand. "Follow me and we'll get you settled," he said motioning to his crew to help Cynthia and Alejandra deboard the seaplane.

CHAPTER 27
EYE OPENING

The door opened and Vic heard shuffling and grunting. The hood over her head prevented her from seeing who was there. She had been sitting in darkness for quite a while since she regained consciousness. However, she had no idea where she was or how long she had been out.

She used meditation techniques to help combat the effects of the tranquilizers. Vic's brain felt like it was trying to run through Jell-O. It was slippery and sticky at the same time. She struggled to hold focus on her thoughts. The fog was slowly lifting and the new information from her senses helped her to break through.

She made out two separate sets of shuffling

285

feet, along with the thud of a pair of boots and the tap of leather-soled shoes on the bare floors. It sounded as though she were being joined by four people, most likely men. Vic heard what she assumed was the sound of a chair being dragged across the floor, followed by more shuffling and grunting.

The hood was pulled off her head and her eyes squinted in the brightness, trying to make out the figures in the room. Through the blinding light, she could see two people sitting in chairs in a circle with her facing in. Vic's eyes quickly scanned the room as she tried to get her bearings and establish her location.

First, she scanned for threats. Her eyes strained to focus.

"Welcome back, Victoria." Leo's greeting expressed his arrogance. He waited patiently and let the sedatives fade away. The other threat was a man in khaki shorts and a lizard print button-down with a rifle standing to her left behind her. She recognized him as the one who had helped put her in restraints while Leo was holding her down.

Next, she identified the others in the chairs... Robby and Camilo! Fear rose as her brain questioned the well-being of the rest of her team. Were they all captured? Killed? Is there anyone left to come to their rescue?

Lastly, she searched for escape options. There were glass doors to a manicured lawn and garden area to her left. Across from her was a hallway, she assumed it led to a living room area. The large mirror on the wall across from her gave her a view of a staircase behind her. It was rare that going upstairs was a good escape route. More often a person fleeing would find themselves trapped. The staircase would be a last resort.

Her senses told her she was in a vacation home somewhere at a great distance from neighbors. The kitchen table had been removed, as well as all items on the counters. She, Camilo, and Robby sat in the middle of the kitchen.

Looking over Leo's shoulder, the tv on the wall flashed a logo as it powered on seemingly by itself. In the mirror, she could see the edge of another tv mounted in the kitchen that was powering on as well. Leo stood with arms folded and a relaxed look on his face. Vic's mind was confused as she watched the image of Ivan with a large grin appear on the screens, Deadpool mug in hand.

"I did it!" Ivan said with a huge grin on his face. "I hacked the servers," he continued. "I know what the Crypto mining and intelligence gathering is about. I know what Leo is doing, and I know all about Leo's cousin, Jamie Alvarado"

Vic's mind was racing to catch up. Looking across at Camilo, he was just as lost as her. Robby looked surprisingly controlled. It seemed as though he was putting the pieces together. Vic shook her head as if the physical motion would shake the things inside into order.

"It is quite impressive that you were able to penetrate our system," Leo shared his respect for Ivan's prowess. "It has protected us from everyone including the CAC to the CIA."

"Waaah," the gag prevented her from being understood.

"Sorry about that beautiful," Leo said, smooth as ever. "I assume you can all keep your voices down." He looked at Robby and Camilo with an eyebrow raised in question. "After all, I'd hate to disturb the neighbors living 2 kilometers away." If there was any question of being able to shout for help, he squashed it.

Leo removed the gags from Camilo and Robby while the other man untied Vic's.

"What..." Vic wasn't even sure what to ask.

Camilo seemed to be at a loss as well and kept

his mouth shut taking in the information and doing his best to make sense of it.

"What do you mean it "protected you from the CAC?" Vic began cautiously. Ivan had given the signal that the connection was secure, but it really didn't make sense with Leo in the room. "I heard you in that room in Ambergris Cay with Goran and Marco," Vic sneered at Leo. "It's obvious you are working for the CAC."

"Well, actually," Ivan interjected, "he is undercover for the CIA." His pride in assembling the pieces was evident on his face.

"Wait... What," Camilo said in disbelief. He was having trouble seeing Leo as anything other than the man he was going to kill for kidnapping his cousin.

"Not for long," Leo said matter-of-factly.

"He's a spook," Camilo questioned, with a pained look on his face.

"Technically, you are all correct," Leo smirked, a bit full of himself. He was able to find success on both sides of the law. That success had gone to his head.

Vic recognized Leo's arrogance and decided to try to toy with him. "So, you're an undercover CIA agent working for Pablo Arias, the head of the

Central American Cartel," Vic said with a sneer. "Qué huevos tenés. You know what he will do if he finds out you're an agent. And yet, you take the assignment gladly."

"What can I say, I enjoy a good challenge," Leo said slowly, looking at Vic as though she were his next conquest.

Vic thought, "Let the games begin."

"So, what are we doing here," Camilo's patience was thinning, and he needed help filling in the big picture.

"Well, you see," Ivan thought it was a good time to try to bridge the gap. "Leo here is interested in retiring from both of his current employers and requests our assistance in doing so."

"What's the problem, the benefits package not acceptable?" Robby's voice was unexpected, especially with the calm witty tone. The look on his face showed that he was following what Ivan and Leo were saying. He was connecting the dots to the current status. It was clear he was a thinker.

Leo looked at Robby quizzically. He was taken aback by how much bolder the man was this time compared to their last encounter. "I have come to find that good and evil exist on both sides of the law. I am tired of being beholden to either."

"What's in it for us," Camilo asked, still unsure how to feel about his status.

Noticing the sun had dropped and was now casting a glare directly in Vic's eyes, Leo walked to the blinds and lowered them to block the glare.

Vic tossed a thankful head nod.

"In helping me, I will help you get in the room with Gregario where you may carry out your vengeance. "Well, not all of you. Robby will need to stay behind; both for his safety and for assurance that you won't double-cross me."

"Are you saying you don't trust me?" Vic said playfully. Camilo picked up on her tactics but that didn't mean that he enjoyed watching it.

"What's your plan?" Camilo said getting back to business.

"Gregario is hosting a dinner where both Pablo Arias and Ron Goldsmith, a corrupt CIA shot caller will be in attendance. I feel that this party will be a great opportunity to proclaim my retirement."

"Are there any other dinner guests we should know about," asked Vic.

"José Gutiérrez, a dirty Mexican official

working with the cartel," answered Ivan. "Guys like this get rich off raping their own country."

"I'm assuming the dinner party is at Gregario's compound outside Matamoros?" Vic asked.

"That's right," confirmed Leo.

"Gregario's compound is sure to be heavily guarded, not to mention additional security for the guests. If you are not on the list, I imagine it would be very difficult to get past security."

"Like trying to sneak into the Grammys," quipped Ivan.

"So how do you propose we get in?" asked Camilo

"He proposes you two go in restrained," Robby said. "He expects to parade the prisoners in like a dog that just retrieved its fetch. He's counting on Gregario's anger toward the prisoners who kidnapped him, who shamed him, who dared put their hands on him, that anger would excuse any interruption. And that's exactly the tactic he will take with the guards."

Leo was surprised that Robby had stolen his thunder.

"So, you want us to go in unarmed," Camilo probed.

"Like lambs to the slaughter," added Vic.

"Well," Leo said guiltily, "I thought maybe we could carry an extra pistol for each of you." That seemed reasonable. In closed-quarters battle, a pistol was often a better weapon than a rifle; and Vic occasionally preferred a knife over a firearm. If a rifle was needed, they could always liberate one from a guard.

"And getting out after it's over?" asked Vic.

"Look, I can go over all the details with you," Leo began his pitch, "but I have to know you are with me before I say too much. I am risking a lot with you. I can tell you that you will not get another chance like this, a chance to be face-to-face with Gregario, not for a long time. He has reinforced his security. He knows you are hunting him, and his men know what you look like. He will be much harder to access than the last time you went after him."

Leo turned and faced Robby and Camilo. "I don't know you to be anything other than honorable men. Robby, I am sorry you have been pulled into this hostile world, but I assure you, I will not harm you. You are safe.

"Great, then you don't mind removing these restraints," said Robby leaning to the side to provide easier access.

Leo did not acknowledge the request, "Camilo, I believe you to be a righteous man who fights for the oppressed. The men in that room are some of the most oppressive and cruel men I have ever heard of. The world will be a better place without them in it."

It was smart to appeal to Camilo's sense of honor and duty. He had seen his share of evil men and he took pride in having extinguished a few of them. Leo was right, he wanted to make the world a better place by hunting down men like this, but how could he trust him?

Camilo looked at Vic who shrugged as if to say, what other options do we have?

"Well, I'm afraid we may be at an impasse," Camilo said. "Because I'm not going to agree to anything until I know all the details. And it's pretty damn tough to be open to what you have to say when we are essentially prisoners."

Robby again leaned to provide access to his wrists. Leo smirked and shrugged, indicating the restraints would stay.

"What is your plan if we say no?" Robby asked.

"I will have to take my chances alone," Leo answered confidently.

"And what happens to us?" Robby probed

further. "You just assured me you would not harm me."

"Oh, you'll be fine," Leo said. "Of course, I can't have you running off and telling anyone of my plans. So, you will have to be my guest until it is finished."

"Guest," Robby challenged. "Do you keep all your guests restrained? If so, you do realize that makes them captives, not guests."

"I know," said Leo. "But guests sound much nicer."

CHAPTER 28

PRISONERS AND PEOPLE OF INTEREST

Vic, Camilo, and Robby were captive "guests" of Leo. He was feeding them the finest cuisine, giving them extensive television entertainment, and would provide various comfort items; but they were confined to their glass cages. The massive glass windows were reclaimed from an aquarium and were several inches thick. However, the cage had an amazing view of the beach. It would be this way until the dinner party.

Leo had allowed the three to meet to discuss their choice to help him or not. It was decided that it was in everyone's best interest to go along with Leo's general plan to eliminate scumbags, but they didn't trust him and needed their own plan for how to get out alive. After the three told Leo they agreed, the three captives, Leo, his cousin Jamie, and Ivan had a planning session. During the video call, Vic used coded messages to instruct Ivan of alternate extract coordinators.

GORDO WAS PLACING a dill pickle slice on his sandwich when the smart TVs on the kitchen and living room walls flickered and displayed a "connecting" icon. A moment later, Ivan's image was displayed. He was finishing a long sip from his Deadpool Mug.

"Uhh... Hi," Gordo was a bit surprised that Ivan had taken over the television. He coughed to indicate his side was secure as well.

The screen split and Priya's feed appeared next to Ivan's

"Hi guys," said Priya cheerfully.

After the long flight, Guayo had been resting on the couch when the impromptu meeting came on the TV. He made his way to the kitchen to join the others. Gordo took the knife and cut his sandwich in half. He passed one of the pieces to Guayo who took it gratefully. He hadn't eaten much in the past twenty-four hours. Guayo opened his mouth wide and took a large bite, leaving a glob of mustard in the corner of his mouth.

"What's up," asked Imri who had just finished taking a bite of his own sandwich. He grabbed his water bottle and washed it down.

"Quite a bit actually," Priya kicked off the meeting. "First off, Ivan has located Vic, Camilo, and Robby."

"They are safe, but..." Ivan trailed off.

"But what?" asked Gordo.

"Leo has them," Ivan said.

"How is that safe?" Imri's voice raised.

"Leo's not who we thought," Ivan began to explain. "The dinner party is not what we thought, we were wrong about a lot."

"What are you saying, Ivan," Gordo asked.

"I hacked the servers, and I was able to see Leo's plan." Ivan continued. "In addition to mining cryptocurrency, they are being used to data mine people. I could take hours going into that but let's shortcut to where I tell you that using that tech to search Leo, I was able to discover that he is an undercover CIA agent assigned to investigate Pablo Arias of the CAC."

"What the..." Imri trailed off.

"CIA, huh," Gordo chimed in. "Well, that figures. Did you contact Vic? What's her status?"

Ivan went on to fill the team in on his call with Vic, Camilo, Robby, Leo, and his associate. It looked more like a group of guys watching a suspense thriller movie than a debriefing, but that's what happens when you interrupt lunch for a group of operators. Guayo reached across for the chips as Imri took another massive bite of his sandwich. Crunching on a pickle, Gordo asked, "So, what's the play?"

"Vic agreed to help Leo with a few modifications to the details of the plan. You three are going to prepare for extract through the tunnel system to your location. On Vic's signal, you will engage the CDG (Gulf Cartel). You will provide cover fire until Vic, Camilo, and Robby are at the rendezvous; and you will escort them out." Ivan proceeded to lay out the plan. The guys listened and made mental notes as they finished their sandwiches and chips.

As they were wrapping up Guayo asked, "Are Alejandra and Cynthia safe?" At that moment Imri recognized the look on his face as he inquired about Alejandra and her daughter. It was clear that Guayo fancied her and there was no doubt about it. He threw a glance at Gordo and back at

Guayo as if to say "Hey, check this out". Gordo whose mind was consumed with the implications of Leo being a fellow agent and hadn't noticed.

"The Skipper reports all is well," interjected Priya who not only was the one following up on the ladies but also noticed Guayo's innocent but special interest in Alejandra. "Alejandra sends her thanks to you and Sr. Gordo for saving her and her Daughter."

Sparing the uncomfortable moment this dialogue was headed for, Gordo said, "Please pass along our best wishes. Is there a plan beyond Brownsville?"

Accepting the pivot, Priya replied, "I am preparing transport and safe passage as we speak and will provide details as I feel they are reliable."

With a plan in place, the team in Brownsville set off to prepare the tunnels to block the cartel from following them. At the least, they hoped they would slow the onslaught of cartel hunters on their tails. They utilized the entire arsenal in one way or another. They planted mines, weapons caches, and traps throughout the exit paths.

As Guayo was preparing a trip wire, Gordo pried, " So, Alejandra, ay?"

Guayo tried to be nonchalant in his response, "What about her?"

"Muy bonito, ¿no?" Gordo pressed.

"Sure, I guess," Guayo answered quickly.

"She seems like a sweet girl," Gordo was doing his best to get Guayo to admit he was attracted to her.

"I didn't spend much time with her, but she seemed kind to me," agreed Guayo. And then he opened up just slightly. "I would not mind getting to know her when this is all over."

Gordo grinned as he saw the cracks in Guayo's shield. "Oh, so you're a romantic," Gordo jested. "No, "hit it and quit it" for you."

"Alejandra is not that kind of woman," Guayo said with a protective tone. "She's the kind of woman you find at church, not at the bar."

"As far as you know," quipped Gordo. "She could be a real party freak; maybe she just hasn't had a lot of opportunities to cut loose.

"I don't think so," Guayo said gruffly.

Gordo could tell Guayo was not wanting to continue this topic. "Anyway, finish up, and let's get back to the third turn. I think it needs more weapons."

. . .

ON THE DAY of the dinner party, Leo allowed Camilo, Robby, and Vic to hang out on the back patio and walk across the beach to the water, under the supervision of his associates of course. Vic had inquired who the associates were, and all Leo would give up is that they worked for Leo, no one else, simply for Leo. On the beach, there wasn't anyone in sight.

Vic sat in the sand with her feet just within the reach of the receding tide. The sand was warm, but the water was cooler than she was used to. The shells were different too. It wasn't "The Gold Coast," but it was beautiful nonetheless. The saltwater felt amazing on Vic's feet.

It was impossible to keep Robby out of the water. Ever since he was a kid, he was the first to get wet. Robby had waded out to float in the gentle waves. Camilo sat next to Vic, just out of reach of the water while taking in the sea air.

"I can't lose him again, Vic" Camilo said, looking out to Robby floating. "We finish the job this time."

"I'm not letting Gregario slip my grasp again," Vic declared. "He will be my first and primary target. As soon as we are out, we will come back for Robby. Are you good with taking out the Mexican official?"

"If Ivan can still be trusted, he's a bad man and it would bring mercy to many," answered Camilo. "Should I still trust Ivan?"

"I've known Ivan a long time, not as long as you, but still. I know hacking Leo's system was a major accomplishment. Ivan is feeling pretty confident right now. He may seem a bit off, but I believe you can trust him. We are like family," Vic assured.

"Well then, No hay problema," said Camilo. "Let's just hope our boys can escort us out."

The pair watched Robby wade in the water. They enjoyed the beautiful day and the beach which, although different than what they were used to, reminded them of home. They sat mostly quietly, enjoying the day. They only shared a few observations and memories of their younger years. They needed the day to take stock to remember why finishing this was necessary.

Leo's associate motioned from the deck that it was time to go. Robby drifted in to join the others on the beach. The trio walked across the sand toward the patio.

"Are you good with this primo?" asked Camilo.

"Are you?" Robby quipped back. "You are the ones going into the wolf den. I just have to hang out and pray you make it out alive."

Camilo threw his arm around his cousin as they made their way back inside. It wasn't much different than the past missions he went on with Vic. He wasn't expected to make it back then and it was no different now. Like Chepe, he would rather go out guns blazing than in a hospital bed. But something told him, if he stuck with Vic, somehow, he would make it back at least mostly in one piece.

Back inside, they prepared to get ready for the night. Robby went to clean up while Vic and Camilo used the sweat, sand, and windblown hair from the beach to help disguise the fine accommodations Leo had provided. During their short stay, Leo had taken quite good care of them with their own private showers and fresh clothing. Vic and Camilo put on the clothes that they were captured in, still dirty from the struggles and transportation.

"Are the two of you ready?" Leo asked.

"Don't worry about us," Camilo responded. "Just get us in the room and we'll handle our part."

"Okay," Leo was impressed by Camilo's

bravado, he was very bold for someone in his position.

"Let's get this over with," Vic's tone was pure business.

Vic and Camilo gave Robby a final hug before one of Leo's men led him back to his room. The other associate climbed in the driver seat of the black Kia Seltos with limousine tint. Leo placed restraints on Vic and Camilo, tight enough to appear effective but loose enough that they could slip them. He put gags in their mouths and bags over their heads to complete the façade of being prisoners, which was still partially true. Leo led them by the arm into the vehicle. Once Vic and Camilo were situated in the back, Leo climbed in the passenger seat, and they drove off.

The trip to Gregario's compound took about forty-five minutes. Vic habitually counted turns and counted the time between, even though she had no point of reference. It wasn't really important; she knew where they were going. She was counting on Ivan to be able to lead them back to Robby. Fortunately, the driver had chosen a decent station to listen to along the drive.

The car slowed and turned onto a smooth

driveway. Ten seconds later it came to a stop. Vic and Camilo sat in anticipation as they waited anxiously for Leo to work his way past the gate guard.

CHAPTER 29
PUT A FORK IN IT

V ic and Camilo were surprised at the ease at which Leo was able to convince the guards to get out of his way. He used logic, reason, and mostly intimidation to force his way deep into the compound. The guards responded out of respect and fear. Fear of Leo, sure. But if not for Leo, they feared what Gregario might do to them and Leo was good at twisting the situation to make the guards look bad if they were not allowed to pass.

The landscape lights began to illuminate with the setting sun. As they climbed the stone steps to the front door, Camilo tripped, and Leo's associate yelled at him to get up. He grabbed Camilo's arm and pulled him to his feet. One of Gregario's guards began to step toward them to offer assistance controlling the prisoners, but with a quick look from Leo, the guard understood that these prisoners were not to be touched.

They made their way through the massive metal front doors that looked like they could take a hit from a mortar and still hold fast. The main house was an impressive work of engineering and art. The structure was built like a bunker with reinforcements throughout and some of the windows were actually bulletproof. The fixtures and furnishings were all extremely tasteful and elegant. There was a mix of old-world Mexican warmth with a modern flare. The bright-colored furnishings offset the darker materials used to create the floors and beams.

Through her hood, Vic could smell the faint scent of floor cleaner just below the cinnamon fragrance from what she assumed to be candles. She could hear the sounds from various boots as she was dragged through the house, but the slap of Leo's leather-soled shoes stood out. Vic used her breathing to stable her nerves and adrenaline. She kept tension on her restraints to help make them appear tighter than they actually were.

The only guards who were holding their

ground were at the door to the dining room. Leo had been announcing that they must see Gregario the entire length of the corridor, but the guards did not step aside. When Leo was close enough, he disarmed the guard, slapped him aside, and kicked in the Bubinga wood door. The other guard surrendered to the mussel of Leo's associate's DDM4 and stepped back from the door.

Leo dragged Vic and his associate pushed Camilo in the back, directing them into the dining room.

"What is this..." Gregario objected to the intrusion.

The guard that was slapped stood in the door and looked to Gregario for direction. Seeing Leo and two hooded figures, Gregario paused. There had to be a good reason he was barging in with prisoners, especially in a meeting with his boss. Arias put his forkful of stuffed poblanos back on his plate and placed his hands under the table. His personal bodyguard stepped up to the back of his chair. The official did not have additional security, he appeared to be startled by the commotion. No doubt, he was already on edge with these two power players of the underworld at the table.

"I've brought a little present, my friend," Leo

answered. He pulled the hoods from Camilo and Vic's heads and Gregario was face to face with his prior captures. Using his white linen napkin, Gregario wiped his mouth, pushed back from the table, and stood up.

"This," Gregario's excitement rose, "this is worth the intrusion."

Turning to Arias he offered his apologies for the interruption.

"My apologies sir, these two are responsible for the disruption in the shipment with the Serbians. And they have offended me personally. My men have been searching for them, yet it looks like your man was able to locate them and bring them to me."

Turning his attention back to Leo, he said, "Thank you for bringing these gifts, I am very grateful."

"It is my pleasure, I assure you," said Leo, turning the corners of his mouth into a large grin.

"Senior Arias, you honor me with these gifts," Gregario said, respecting that Leo worked for Pablo and as such the gift came from his house.

"Oh, these are not from him," Leo said with a lack of respect that raised the eyebrows of the men at the table. "These are from me to you; I have a different gift for Senior Arias, but we will get to that in a moment." They did not expect this insubordinate tone and were not the type of men who enjoyed games.

"Leo, what is the meaning of this?" Pablo asked gruffly.

"Well, you see," Leo tapped the side of Vic's foot with his heel and looked at his associate and Camilo to signal to get ready to attack. "I am giving you my resignation and I could not think of a better place than this.

Pablo's expression reflected his rising anger. First, you do not simply resign from the Central American Cartel. Second, you do not attempt it publicly where you will bring disgrace to the organization. This was an embarrassment.

Gregario wasn't going to allow this disrespect in his house. As great as the gift of the prisoners was, it was not worth the price of insulting his guests, especially not Senior Arias. "Just bring me that whore and her sidekick and be gone. Senior, I will let you address this issue in a more appropriate setting." He tried to help Pablo save face.

It was go time.

"Yu..Fu.." Vic tried to yell at Gregario through her gag.

Leo turned and punched her in the gut, or at least it looked like a punch. Vic doubled over with the "punch", slipping her restraints she quickly grabbed the knife that was strapped inside the leg of Leo's pants. Leo drew his weapon and pointed it at Pablo while his associate spun around to the guards at the door behind them. Camilo stripped his restraints and pulled the pistol from the associate's shoulder holster and took aim at the Mexican Official.

The men at the table froze, trying to understand what was happening. Vic lunged for Gregario. Pablo's bodyguard began to pull his weapon and Leo dropped him with a headshot between the eyebrows. Leo's associate opened fire on the guards at the door who fell back into the corridor from the force of the bullets.

It was only a matter of moments before the security forces would descend on the room. Reinforcements would be called and all members in Matamoros would be put on alert. The more time they spent, the stronger the opposing forces would become. They had to move fast.

Vic took three steps into the center of the U-shaped table before leaping across the middle to reach Gregario. Her spandex leggings slid across the silk tablecloth like a slip-and-slide. She led with her running shoe, the heel of which caught Gregario squarely in the jaw sending him tumbling over his chair. Landing on his back, he regained focus just in time to look into Vic's eyes as she sliced his throat with the blade.

A blast came from under the table and splinters of the table blew past the right side of Leo's head. Pablo had fired a shot from the revolver he was holding under the table. Leo and Camilo fired simultaneously and the heads of the Mexican official and Pablo whipped backward from perfect headshots.

Vic pulled the gag from her mouth and reached her hand out toward Leo. Leo reached into his pocket and pulled out two in-ear coms units. He handed one to Vic and put the other in his own ear. His associate did the same with Camilo who had turned with him to cover the door.

Vic inserted her coms and announced, "Room clear, get us out of here."

"Take the door in the right back corner to the kitchen." Ivan was using the digital schematics of the compound to guide the team through the maze of the house with the fewest guards to the rendezvous point. Leo's cousin Jaime had created the plans with the program installed on the servers. The program used the smart devices like phones and watches of the guards, service people, and even Gregario to not only map out the compound, but the AI was able to predict where each individual would be based on habits and historic data. The server room Vic had stumbled on was going to help keep her alive.

Camilo stepped into the doorway and liberated an AK from one of the door guards. As soon as he had it in his hand a pair of guards rounded the corner of the corridor and Camilo squeezed the trigger. He stepped back into a defensive posture and dropped the left guard as Leo's associate put three rounds in the one on the right. The pair backed into the room and Camilo spoke up, "Time to move."

The unit followed Vic through the door on the right into the kitchen. Leo and Vic covered the front while Camilo and the associate leapfrogged covering the rear. Vic and Leo moved through the space and around each other like a well-choreographed dance. The kitchen staff had panicked at the sound of gunfire and only a few were still making their way out of the kitchen. There was a guard who had appeared through the door next to the walk-in freezer. Vic threw the carving fork from the counter, and it lodged in his esophagus. She grabbed the guard's gun and left the fork in his neck.

Ivan was using the transmitter in the coms to track each of the team members. "To the right again. That door will lead to the hallway."

While Ivan was navigating the team, Priya had hacked Gregario's security feed and was monitoring the cameras throughout the compound. "A truckload of men just arrived at the front gate. More are on their way. The guards at the back wall have doubled." In addition to the cameras, Priya was also managing the extraction team. "X team is at the extraction point standing by."

Camilo and the associate managed a small surge from the back. Camilo shot a guard in the kneecap which created an obstacle that held the others up for a moment. They took advantage of the opportunity and caught up with Vic and Leo as they entered the hallway.

Vic swung the M&P AR-15 she lifted off the guard to the left and dropped low while Leo stood straight and fired his Sig Sauer P220 to the right. The crack, pop, and bang of the bullets firing, and shrapnel was deafening. The hallway with mahogany arches to the vaulted ceiling reverberated the sound. Three down on the left and two on the right. The four stepped into the hallway and ensured it was clear.

"Left down the hallway to the end of the hall, then right." Ivan directed.

"How big is this fucking house?" Camilo asked under his breath.

"Big enough," Leo whispered back.

Hot brass poked at the sole of Vic's running shoe as they made their way down the hall. It was unfortunate that she was captured while running, a pair of boots would be really nice right about now.

Another small group of guards appeared at the end of the hall behind them. The associate and Camilo set up defensive positions behind a couple of pillars that were holding plants and began cover fire. Leo and Vic sprinted for the corner and turned back to cover the other's retreat.

Before advancing to the hallway, Camilo and the associate were able to drop three of the five. They took over Leo and Vic's positions of defending from the corner. Vic and Leo ran toward the door at the end of the hall.

"Through that door is trouble but it's your only option," said Ivan in a dry tone.

The associate was able to hit each of the remaining guards pursuing in the hallway and he and Camilo raced to join Leo and Vic at the door.

"The guards from the trucks are coming in the front door," Priya updated.

CHAPTER 30
SHOWERED IN FLOWER PETALS AND LEAD

"X team, GO!" ordered Ivan.

The wall on the west end of the property blew and the guards dropped. Imri dropped the guard on the outside of the door, sniping from the tree line.

"Now, Vic." Ivan followed up.

Leo followed Vic out the door and covered the left as she took the right. Leo's associate took over the right and Camilo the left. Leo and Vic changed focus toward the hole in the wall. Cartel men were filing in from both sides of the building. They had to make a run for it.

Gordo and Guayo covered the exit through the wall. They located and eliminated guards like machines. Gordo was focused on the guards coming from the right and Guayo from the left. Imri continued to acquire and destroy targets from his perch, clearing the path to the wall.

Vic led the team off the back porch and down through the gardens. They took turns covering their escape as they moved tactically toward the wall. Petals of flowers showered them as bullets from their trailers fired into the beautifully manicured Bougainvillea. The squad raced through the opening and put their backs to the wall to catch their breath. Gordo spotted Leo's associate, grabbed him by the chest, and pinned him to the wall.

"What are you doing here?" Gordo said forcefully. It was clear he knew the man.

"He's with me," Leo interjected.

"He helped us get Gregario and got us out of there," Vic said.

Gordo shook his head as if to clear it. He knew they had to move, or they would all be dead. He would deal with this guy later. "Follow me!"

The six made their way to the tree line, taking fire the entire way. Imri had done a great job dropping bodies in the wall opening. As soon as he had crosshairs aligned, he would pull the trigger. His Scout Squad M1A-A1 had run through 5 ten-round magazines already. Imri's resistance had given them a 23-second lead by the time the others reached him.

"SUVs are closing in from the southwest," Priya alerted.

"We've got to move!" Gordo said hastily. He left the tree line and turned down a road that dead-ended at Gregario's property. There were several housing units and shops. It was early evening so many people were on the streets. The seven tried to conceal their weapons to avoid causing a scene, as they rushed down alleys and streets toward the shop.

On a street three blocks from Gregario's compound was a convenience shop. Behind that shop was a small storage shed. There was a hole in the floor of the shed that accessed the tunnel system. The team had to get to the tunnels before the cartel men got to them. Once they reached the tunnels, they had the advantage over the cartel and should easily be able to escape.

Guayo stepped forward and took point with Vic next to him, followed by Camilo. Their skin tone did not stand out like Gordo or Imri, and they spoke Spanish in case civilians became an issue. The woman in running clothes somehow disarmed people and it drew the people's attention away from the gringos with guns behind her. Vic ran her hand over her braids which had begun to unravel a bit. Her body was something to look at, but her head was a bit of a dirty mess. It didn't matter, few took the time to look at her head, their focus was a bit lower.

Only a few people noticed the weapons, but no one did anything about it. In this neighborhood, it was not unusual to see armed men. One wannabe tough guy began to step up when he noticed Guayo's weapon, but a quick scan at the others with him made him reconsider. Gordo looked back to see him calling someone on his phone. They needed to get off the streets. Chances are whoever he was calling would relay their location and the cartel would be all over them.

A couple of alleys and one busy sidewalk later, they arrived at the convenience store. Guayo posted up on the corner and peered around to make sure the coast was clear. He turned to Vic and nodded with a smile. "Time to go underground".

End of part 2

FREE READ: SHE'S BACK FOR REDEMPTION

Continue the journey, and grab the first three chapters for free - Victoria Villalobos Redemption.

Free Read: Redemption

Victoria Villalobos Series

Enter the world of Victoria Villalobos and experience the ultimate journey of redemption and self-discovery. Follow Victoria and her allies as they face impossible challenges, heart-pumping action, and gripping suspense in this thrilling series. With each book, you'll be drawn deeper into the story and the characters, rooting for them every step of the way. Join the adventure and get hooked on the Victoria Villalobos series today!

ABOUT THE AUTHOR

 Steve Page is a bestselling author of multiple books, including Cut The Crap & Move To Costa Rica and The Ultimate Costa Rica Cookbook. Expanded his writing into the world of fiction with his first crime novel Victoria Villalobos: Retribution. He is the president of Viva Purpose Inc., an international publishing company. He is a speaker, and coach who has helped numerous people around the world transform their personal and professional lives.

Steve uses his technical and entrepreneurial experience to help other authors and entrepreneurs find personal and professional success. He loves to share his entrepreneurial knowledge and imagination with his readers.

Through his websites, blogs, and social media, Steve continues to provide expert advice to relocators, with current events and the logistics of nomad and expat life. He also helps independent authors self-publish and promote their books with both training courses and mentorship. Steve continues to travel abroad and enjoys his life.

Author Page

Visit Steve Page's author page for the latest information on new releases.

Steve Page: Author Page

You may enjoy some of our content on our websites:

www.vivapurpose.com

www.cutthecrapcostarica.com

www.theultimatecostarica.com